3001

Ginger Lee

ISBN 978-0-578-69307-1 (paperback)
ISBN 978-1-7350544-0-7 (ebook)

Cover design by Deranged Doctor Design (https://www.derangeddoctordesign.com).

Editing by Augustin Kendall, Clarify Editing (http://www.clarify-editing.com/).

Interior formatting and design by Janell E. Robisch, Speculations Editing (https://speculationsediting.com).

For Brian and Alex Jane

CONTENTS

CHAPTER ONE

There were two routes. One wound from north to south, the other from west to east. The ancient tunnels twisted through Freywood Mountain. At its heart flickered an ever-burning fire. It marked the exact middle; the Crossroads deep inside the earth. The light from the fire lit up the huge cavern, as large as a small city, which served as a rest stop for travelers. Hustle and bustle was all around. Merchants bartered from tents full of food and supplies for sale or trade. Traveling musicians played jolly music beside the tavern, everyone's favorite spot to stop for a drink or a card game. Years ago, someone had built cabins for a good night's rest.

Rory Larken was an innkeeper of sorts. She kept the sleeping quarters clean, did laundry, and made a hearty breakfast for those who stayed. At only thirty years of age, Rory was a widow. She had lived in the middle of the mountain since her husband, Shaw, passed away ten years before. The loss left her alone, and she needed a warm, safe home where she could earn a livelihood. Winters could be bitter in Freywood, and she never worried about freezing so far from the outside. Rory wasn't even sure she could freeze. Even though she was strikingly beautiful, with pale skin and hair as bright as the sun, she had never remarried. There was a peculiarity about her. Others who lived in the cavern whispered about her differences, but they were never spoken of aloud.

Her ability made her vital to those around her. The fire that never extinguished, the source of light and heat for so many, was perpetuated by Rory's own hand.

Since childhood, she had felt an electricity, a vibrating running through her body. She never met her father, but her mother always told her this ability came from him. Her mother would not tell her why her father had left before she was born, but he had passed on some of himself to her. Rory had not known why, but she now made use of it after a personal tragedy on the outside.

Ten years ago, she became sick with a life-threatening fever. As a child, she often had an above-average body temperature, but this was a first. She had never suffered any childhood sickness.

Afraid of her getting worse, Shaw ventured out in the evening to harvest arrowroot to break the fever. As he returned, he smelled a hint of smoke, then noticed the glow of a fire on the other side of the hill. Only, it was too large for a campfire. Their small home blazed, engulfed in flames. Shaw threw down everything he carried and ran into the burning cabin. Rory's body lay untouched by fire. He got the window open next to the burning bed and managed to get his wife through, but he didn't make it out.

Rory knew what had sparked the fire. The same spark that kept the Eternal Flame alive. After what she had done, she dedicated herself to never ending any kind of life again, human or animal. She became careful and consumed arrowroot daily to stave off another high fever.

Her predecessor, a lumberjack, had kept the flame thriving in the usual ways. He was very old when she made her way to the middle of the mountain. She needed to be useful, and he was more than happy to retire his role. She had resided at the Crossroads ever since.

2

A fellow named Lawson drove the wet wagon through every evening with a fresh supply of water from the falls located on the south side of the mountain. Rory used a lot of water doing laundry, cooking, and bathing, so she traded for her share. Lawson left a sack of his dirty clothes and blankets to swap for the ones she washed for him. Thus, a daily routine began. She also gave him any leftovers from breakfast after the children of the cavern dwellers had their fill.

For the first few years she resided in the hidden city, he attempted to woo her. He was nice-looking enough, and they shared many conversations about mutual interests, but Rory had no deep feelings for him.

She also didn't trust herself not to hurt another person. Each night, she poured her bathwater into a small moat that encircled her tent to guard against another incident. She learned to control her spark as far as she could tell, but she couldn't be too careful.

✺✺✺✦✺✺✺

Rory lay fast asleep one winter's eve when she was awakened suddenly in the middle of the night. The seamstress, Lilian, shook her shoulders.

"There's a man! His poor horse brought him to the Eternal Flame. He's almost frozen to death! Can you help him?" she begged.

Rory slid her dress over her head and ran after her.

A group of healers, who always stopped to stay for the harshest part of the winter, encircled the man beside the fire. They had stripped him down to his underpants because his garments were covered with a thick layer of snow and ice. The fire melted the ice from his dark hair and beard, but his lids stayed shut.

Rory could see that his chest barely rose and fell as he took shallow breaths. The oldest healer and one of Rory's only confidants, Nigel, worked at finding a healthy pulse.

He shouted to the crowd that gathered, "Macon! Bring me your strongest ale!"

The tavern keeper ran for his special concoction. The healer knew of Rory's capabilities and motioned for her. As she kneeled over the tall man, Rory laid her hands on his cold cheeks. He let out a pain-filled moan.

Without reservation, she ordered, "Help me lift him."

The men obeyed and she scooted underneath as they laid his upper body in her lap. Her warm arms wrapped around his shoulders. Tears threatened to spill from her eyes; she was afraid he wouldn't make it.

Macon handed the bottle over, and Nigel poured generously.

Rory whispered in the stranger's ear, "Drink, my friend. We are going to bring you back."

He took the entire bottle.

Nigel asked her quietly, "Is there an empty cabin? We need to get him into a warm bed, and you need to lie with him."

Rory stared wide-eyed.

He understood her expression and assured her, "You can save him. There's no one else. Only you can do this. I will explain to the others. Don't worry, my dear. They will understand."

She nodded in acceptance.

They gathered him up on a sled and pulled him to a cabin. Nervously shifting her weight from one foot to the other, Rory waited outside while Nigel and his companion, Renfroe, undressed the man and placed him in the bed. Renfroe handed her another bottle of ale and sent her in.

The windows were covered with muslin. Flames crackled in the small fireplace. Rory had not been naked with a man since Shaw, but this was necessary. She crawled in behind him and pressed the

4

length of her body against his freezing one. She put her cheek on his, held his large cold hand in her hot one, and wrapped her leg over his hip. Her body vibrated against him, surprising her. The sensation was a first. Rory emitted heat from her head to her toes, and he responded quickly. His breathing returned to a normal rhythm and she felt his heartbeat strengthen.

After about an hour, he began to make noises. She thought she heard him whispering and propped up to hear him better over his shoulder.

His voice was hoarse. "Don't worry. I know."

She responded, "Sir? Are you okay? Are you feeling better? What do you know?"

He replied, deeper, louder now, "I know why you are here. Why you have to do this for me, and I'm very thankful. You saved my life, I think. You didn't have to, but you did."

She soothingly hushed him. "You need your rest. I need to stoke the fire. Are you warm enough? Feels like you are."

"Yes, thanks to you."

"Let me get dressed. Don't turn over yet."

After a moment, she added wood to the fire and threw a few sparks in, then spoke. "Okay. Would you like to sit up? Do you remember the last time you ate anything?"

He groaned and scooted upright. "Not really. I think I could eat my horse, though. I'm guessing he's still alive, since I'm here."

She walked over and pulled the wool blanket up, covering his well-defined chest.

"Yes. That horse of yours is the real hero. He's being treated like royalty, I'm sure."

She padded over to the door and cracked it open to see the pair of healers leaned upon each other, asleep on a bench. The couple always wore brightly colored robes that flattered their brown skin. The two kept their dark brown eyes lined with black paint. They loved each other very much and were seldom seen apart.

She touched the nearest shoulder. "Nigel, he's awake and doing well, but we need to feed him. His name ... we don't even know his name."

Nigel hurried away to the tavern, which was always open. They served a hearty stew, perfect to satisfy the no-name stranger.

Each cabin had a tub, and Rory trotted off toward the water tank. It had to be nearing morning, and she figured the man would benefit from a hot bath. She enlisted the help of the stable hands to gather buckets of water and instructed them to bring them in.

Nigel met her back at the door and handed her a tray of food and more ale.

"Don't you want to check him over?"

"Oh, I trust he's in good hands, my dear," he replied with a wink.

He turned and motioned for Renfroe to follow as they made their way back to the tavern. Rory entered and sat the tray on the table beside the bed. She lit the lamp with the touch of her fingers.

Three young men filled up the tub. Rory eased down beside the man, broke off some bread, and handed it to him.

"What's your name?" she asked.

"Jacoby. What's yours?"

"I'm Rory. I'm what you would call an innkeeper."

He smiled knowingly.

"I think you're a lot more than an innkeeper," he said, gesturing over to the lamp.

The tub was full, and they were alone again. She wasn't sure why, but she was exposing herself totally to this man. She placed the tray in his lap and went to stand over the water.

6

"After you eat, you can get a good, thorough cleaning. Watch this."

She let her palms hover over the surface. As Jacoby filled his stomach, he watched the water begin to boil in awe. She dipped both hands into a bucket of cool water when she was done. She panted and took a few deep breaths.

"Amazing!"

"The stew?" she joked, but the smile left her face. "The others don't talk about it. They know what I'm capable of, but it's never discussed, at least not to my face. That's why the healers brought me to you. I've never shown that to anyone before." She pointed to the hot water.

"I guess you've experienced what I can do intimately. Are you married? It doesn't matter really, but I would feel better if you weren't."

He sat the tray down and swung his feet off the bed, keeping the blanket over his lap.

"No. One day, I hope."

He was the finest specimen of a man she had ever seen. He would tower over the other men here, and his features were all male, yet beautiful at the same time. His voice stirred something inside her.

"You ready for a dip?" She reached over, grabbed a pillow, and placed it in his lap.

"Hold on to this. I'll help you over there."

Jacoby held the pillow with one hand, and she held the other.

"Your hand. It's not hot now. You control it well?" he questioned.

"Yes. I've learned the mind is a powerful thing."

She handed him a chunk of goat-milk soap, took a towel from the dresser, and placed it beside the tub.

"I'll leave you be for a little bit. I'm going to wash your clothes. It won't take me long. If you feel up to it, we can go check on your horse."

7

He stepped into the soothing water, and she stepped outside.

❖❖❖❖❖❖

Lilian's daughter, Shannon, already stood at the wash-basin cleaning Jacoby's clothes along with those of the others staying in the cabins.

"Morning, Rory! I figured you'd been up half the night and could use some help. I also heard the stranger is very handsome. You know there's a short-age of good-looking, available men around here. I want to make a good first impression. I wish to make a good wife one day."

Shannon was eighteen and more than ready to marry. She was beautiful, kind, and a hard worker. Rory liked her but felt a twinge of jealousy arise. She internally scolded herself. She had no right to deny the young girl the opportunity to find love.

"Is he? Handsome? You would know ..." she asked secretively, like the topic was forbidden.

"Yes. Very. Now, let me dry his clothes quickly, so he won't be walking around here naked."

Rory laughed. She noticed his clothes were a bit unusual. They were so well made that she couldn't fathom how a seamstress accomplished such perfect stitching.

"Why don't you bake him something sweet and give it to him tonight at the tavern?" she suggested to Shannon.

"Oh, yes! I know just what to make," she replied.

Rory headed back to the cabin. She knocked before going on in. He sat by the fire with the towel wrapped around his waist.

"You look lively. Are you okay?" she asked with a warm smile. He did look amazing, considering his condition only hours before.

"I can't believe how good I feel. I think it was you," he said seriously.

"Me?" Rory was feeling nervous for the first time around him. "I just warmed you up and fed you," she said meekly.

He lightened the mood. "Well, I wouldn't be here without you. This place. It's the Crossroads, right? I passed through, but that was a long time ago. I'd love a shave. You have a barber, don't you?"

She nodded. "As a matter of fact, we do. Hal can take care of you. We can stop there before we go to the stable."

Rory watched Hal delicately use a short blade to remove the black beard. She cringed with every swipe, thankful when it was over. Jacoby looked at least five years younger. Maybe he wasn't too old for Shannon.

He rubbed his perfect jaw. "So?" he asked, looking dashing.

Her stomach did a flip. "You look like a prince."

She questioned him outside as they walked to the horse stalls. "Are you? A prince? I've never seen the prince of Freywood. You could be him."

He shook his head. "Not I, my fair maiden. I'm a bounty hunter, among other titles. You see, I was commissioned by the king of Freywood to kill the ... group of dragons that killed his livestock and soldiers this past summer. The very same dragons that terrorized three other cities. They tend to hide in cave dwellings during the winter, so I made my move when I knew they would least expect it. I will spare you the gory details, but I was successful. I waited too long, though. A terrible freezing storm pushed its way through right when I tried to get back. I should have waited it out a bit, but I didn't, and you know, it almost killed me.

"Imagine surviving a battle with dragons only to suffer death by the cold." He laughed. "That would be tragic."

9

Jacoby's black horse was the biggest Rory had ever seen. He had been groomed and fed. The way Jacoby touched the beast, she could tell they were close companions. Nigel walked in with Renfroe in tow and shook Jacoby's hand.

"My good man! You survived! Ah, our Rory did the trick. Sir, you must stop by my tent. I need to check you over, and although you miraculously didn't get frostbite, I have some salve that will soothe your muscles."

He turned to Rory. "My dear, you must go. Sleep, bathe, and join us at the tavern for dinner."

She had to admit, she was about to pass out.

Jacoby took her hand and kissed it. "I'll save you a seat beside me."

Rory blushed, gave a bow, and went on her way. She took a cool bath and slept longer than she had planned.

Rory woke and put on her favorite dress. It was deep red velvet and tied in a tight corset at the waist. The supple fabric dipped lower in the front than her other dresses, showing a tasteful hint of her ample curves. She had never worn the garment in public or called attention to her beauty before.

Rory paused on the porch of the tavern to peek inside before she went in. Jacoby sat at a long table surrounded by several of the cavern's single women. He oozed charm. They were all having a good time. She figured he had already consumed several mugs of ale. She couldn't blame him. He had cheated death and lived to tell his warrior tales. Shannon, close by his side, fed him berry cobbler.

Nigel and Renfroe walked up the steps behind her. "Oh, my lovely, lovely! Oh, Rory! You will break many hearts, my dear."

"You are too sweet, Nigel. That's not my plan."

He winked at her. "Maybe just one, huh, my dear?"

She entered with the couple, and all eyes were on her. She swallowed hard and looked at Jacoby. He stood up, much to the ladies' dismay. Rory nodded hello to him and started to sit at a small table by the door.

"Rory! No, no. Girls, if you please, make a spot for Rory. She's with me tonight."

They all whined a bit but obeyed. Shannon stayed put on one side.

Rory walked over and announced, "It's okay, ladies. There's enough of Jacoby to go around. Am I right?"

The whole room laughed, and the girls agreed. The party resumed. She was starving and enjoyed her dinner while listening to endless questions from the women. After she had some of Shannon's cobbler, Jacoby asked her to join him by the fire. They sat on a small bench only big enough for two, facing the firelight.

"Ah, I needed a break. Thank you," he said, brushing his dark hair away from his thick brows.

She smiled. "Are you tired? I'm sure Nigel would make a spectacle and send you to bed if you want to get out of here."

"Tempting ... but I don't mind your company."

She felt a vibration in her core. She didn't know why this man affected her this way. She told herself it was only his deep soothing voice and not the look in his eyes.

"Well, I'm happy to sit with you and not be bothersome."

He leaned nearer and said in a low tone only she could hear, "I feel your energy. It amazes me. I'm so intrigued by you. I've talked so much about myself tonight. Would you tell me about yourself?"

She figured she may as well. He had seen her in a way no one else in the settlement had. She told him all there was to tell, from growing up next to the waterfalls to losing Shaw after only one year of marriage.

"That's why I have kept to myself all these years. I keep busy, and I'm happy to be somewhat accepted." She looked down at her hands.

She was the prettiest thing he'd ever seen, and her sweet spirit pulled at his somewhat tortured one.

He sensed a bit of sadness in her tone. "I imagine it's a little lonely. I mean, I know how it feels to be on your own. I tend to keep to myself, even when there are multitudes around me. Well, except for Toby. That's my horse. Excellent conversationalist."

He made her laugh.

Shannon appeared and grabbed Jacoby by the hand. She pulled him to his feet, saying in a childish voice, "Good sir, please come dance!" He reluctantly followed.

The firelight faded, so Rory threw a spark on the wood, and with the small wave of her hand the flames grew bright again. No one noticed. The focus of the room was on Jacoby and the giggling Shannon. He twirled the girl around the room. Rory settled at a small table with Nigel and Renfroe.

When one song ended, another girl stepped in for a whirl. Each time they circled near Rory, Jacoby made funny faces. He mocked being in pain and begged to be rescued.

After several women took their turns, she couldn't leave him hanging any longer. She jumped to the front of the line just as a lone violin began to play a slow, moody tune. Jacoby was almost out of breath and mouthed the words "thank you" as he placed his hand on her waist. He watched her put her hand in his intently. Her beautiful, slender fingers wrapped around his large ones, and the heat and vibration felt like a drug shared between them. It instantly calmed him. He had never been so close to anyone like her. As they swayed together, neither wanted to let go.

He looked down at her, and she admitted, "I haven't had this much human contact in a decade."

He smiled with sympathetic eyes. "Every living thing should be touched, loved, taken care of. Solitude is only good for a person in small servings."

She looked down at her hand resting on his heart, feeling it beat. "I have to admit, this is nice."

When she looked back up, his face was so close to hers. She almost forgot the crowd around them. The song ended and she stepped out of his embrace. Shannon appeared again, ready to reclaim him.

"One more bit of cobbler, then I'm off to bed," he declared. Rory slipped out and went to her tent.

CHAPTER TWO

She found it difficult to settle down and go to bed. She had already slept too much earlier, and her mind raced. She yearned for more human contact. Her thoughts were on Jacoby and Shannon. It made complete sense for them to be interested in one another. Rory told herself she only felt a bond to Jacoby because of the unfortunate circumstance he'd been in the night before.

Obvious footsteps neared the outside of her tent, and she secretly wished it were Jacoby coming to find her.

A familiar female voice whispered, "Rory! Are you awake? Rory?"

Rory opened the flap. "Yes, Shannon. What are you doing? Is everything all right?"

The girl invited herself inside and plopped down on Rory's bed. She beamed. "It's wonderful! I had the best time tonight! Jacoby loved my cobbler, and he's the best dancer. Isn't he the best?"

Rory smiled. "Yes. I like him a lot. He's very brave and very handsome."

Shannon looked concerned. "You're not in love with him, are you?"

Rory laughed at the idea. "Shannon! I have no claim on Jacoby. We've only just met him, and I don't believe he will be staying around long."

The girl started to pout, disappointed. "He left the tavern before I could ask him to walk me to my tent."

Rory sighed inside, inwardly thankful. She had imagined the two cuddled up, kissing behind the cabins like young lovers.

Tired of thinking about it, she helped Shannon toward the door. "It's getting late. You need to get your beauty sleep. I may need laundry help in the morning."

Shannon nodded and went on her way. Rory ate a few bits of arrowroot and a hand full of nettie berries to help her sleep. Within an hour, she was out.

❊❊❊❊❊

First thing in the morning, Rory headed to the tavern to help Macon cook breakfast. The smell of tenderloin and eggs never failed to wake up the whole town. The farmers who settled at the Crossroads raised sheep for wool, chickens for eggs, pigs for meat, and goats for milk to make soap and cheese. Animals were only kept inside the mountain during the winter. They had large farms on the west side of the mountain for the other seasons.

Shannon stopped by just long enough to tell her she would take care of the laundry. Jacoby came in a few minutes after Shannon had gone. He sat at a table, and Rory dished up a large portion of food for his breakfast. She set it in front of him, and he grabbed hold of her hand. Small electrical pulses flowed from her palm to his. She eased down in the chair across from him.

He whispered, "Does this happen with anyone else?"

At a loss for words, she let out a breath.

"I'm guessing that's a no."

She cleared her throat. "Really, I'm not sure how or why this is happening."

He frowned. "Last night I had to sneak out of here to get away from Shannon. Did you sneak out to get away from me?"

Rory took her hand from his and placed it in her lap. "Jacoby, I don't want to sneak away from you. I don't know why I did it. I guess I didn't want to get in the way of your good time. You and Shannon seemed to be getting along, and—"

He held up a hand to stop her. "Me and Shannon? Shannon is ... she's beautiful and very young. It's not like that from me. I'm not the man for her."

Rory wasn't sure how to respond. He leaned across the table a bit closer to her and closed his eyes.

In a low tone he said, "Even when I'm not touching you, I feel you near me. It has to mean something."

His heavy green eyes opened. "That blood-red dress you were wearing last night ... it was stunning."

Rory blushed, and couldn't help but smile. "Jacoby ..."

"Call me Jake." He broke from the intimate words. "You want to join me at the stables?" he asked.

"Okay. I'm sure Toby is missing you."

✣✣✣✣✣✣

Rory pulled a carrot from her apron pocket and fed it to the stallion while Jacoby dug through his saddle-bags. He retrieved a metallic box and unlocked it with a key that hung from a chain on his belt.

"In about a week or maybe less, we should get a break from the snow for a few days. Spring is coming. I will be delivering this to the king."

He opened the lid. Inside were two halves of a black heart. Rory thought it looked a little small, but knew it had to be a dragon's heart.

He continued. "The king of Freywood and the other two city leaders owe me rewards for defeating them. This is the proof I must provide."

"What kind of reward? Money doesn't mean a lot these days. What you've done should be worth something special."

He laughed. "Yes. I have asked for different commodities from each one. King Whitlow has promised an entire library of books."

Rory's eyes lit up with excitement. "Books? But how? I've only seen a few in my lifetime!"

"Each kingdom has scavenger parties, as does the city I come from. They venture to every possible vacant place to look for medical supplies, food, clothing, and curiosities from days past."

She looked thoroughly confused.

"Rory, for your entire life, all you have known is only a tiny fraction of what has been and what is at present. You've only lived around this mountain and Freywood castle that sits on top of the mountain. There is an entire world out there. I've seen a lot of it. Some inhabitants are friendly. Some are not so peaceful. There is a city, a colony called the Briar. It's wonderful. They have so many innovations and buildings you wouldn't believe existed unless you saw them. I have lived there most of my adult life and helped improve their military. Sorry, that's the soldiers who protect the colony. The people look up to me and have asked that I become what's called the governor."

Rory stumbled to find the words to say, "It sounds like something out of a dream."

Jacoby encouraged her. "Why don't you come with me? You could at least accompany me up the mountain. Then, if you didn't want to go any further, I could leave you back here on my way to the Briar."

She shook her head. "The dwellers depend on me so much, and I keep the fire going ..."

"You haven't always been around. The men can make fire if it's necessary. Do you mean to stay here forever?"

She didn't want to get too excited about the possibility of new adventures, but she couldn't help it. Her huge smile showed all her teeth. Hot tears formed in her eyes and slid down her face. "I would give anything to experience what has been unknown to me."

Jacoby took both her hands in his, feeling her warm vibrations. "So you will come with me?"

She hesitated. "What about ... you know? What if I lose control, or, I don't know ..." She looked down at his hands grasping hers. He let go of one, lifted her chin, and assured her, "I will protect you. We won't tell anyone. You're strong. Remember, you can always come back here. It only takes a full day to reach Frey-wood castle."

Rory felt like a freed bird. "Okay. I will go with you."

Rory and Jacoby went about the next few days like there were no plans to leave together. The only person she truly trusted was Nigel. He had mentioned before that he and Renfroe would like to stop traveling and stay put at the Crossroads. Rory asked him to meet her at the tavern for dinner the evening before they were to go.

After Rory explained the situation, Nigel smiled. "My dear, my wish is to live the rest of my days here inside the mountain. I'm sure young Shannon would help out with the guests. Ren and I know how to take care of the Eternal Flame."

He held her hands. They felt hot but did not emit the same pulses she shared with Jacoby.

"Rory, I've never believed that keeping a fire alive was your only purpose in this big world. There are many wonders you should see, and there may even be more like you." He winked. The thought hadn't occurred to her before, even though her father had to have relatives somewhere.

She smiled at her dear friend. "Thank you. I can never repay you. Wish me luck. The snow has ceased, so we are heading out right before the sun rises."

❊❊❊❊❊

After dinner, Nigel took a medical pack bound with twine to Jacoby's cabin.

He shook the younger man's hand. "Rory knows what to do with everything in the pack. I pray you won't need any of it. She's special, Jake. Keep her safe. She's like a daughter to Ren and me."

Jacoby grabbed onto the healer's hand with both of his. "I know. She holds you in the highest regard. And ... I know she is a rare and beautiful creature who has made a profound impact on me. I will not let you or her down. We will send word back to you if she chooses to journey with me to the Briar."

After the older man left, Jacoby lay on the small cabin bed. His thoughts drifted to Rory. He never imagined he'd be so close to a female half. Something he couldn't quite put his finger on drew them together. There were halves in the army and on the flight team at the Briar, but none were really his friends. A brief sadness took hold as he admitted to himself that he didn't have anyone he counted on more than acquaintances, the soldiers who worked with him, and the occasional female companion. The humans and halves of the colony looked up to him as a leader and nothing more, only because he closed himself off to others, and he knew it deep down.

❊❊❊❊❊❊

Toby's stall held all they had gathered for the trip. They met while it was still dark outside. Jacoby made alterations to the saddle to accommodate Rory comfortably. It was still almost freezing, but they both knew there was no worry with her to keep them warm. A sled carried the load behind the horse. Jacoby hopped up into the saddle and hauled Rory up to sit behind him. She wrapped a wool blanket around them both and slid her arms around his waist.

Toby took them down the shortest route through the western tunnel. They reached the opening at sunrise. The falls gleamed in the sun, almost frozen in time with only a small steady stream flowing downward to the ice-covered pool beneath. A clear trail wound up the side of the mountain—a direct path to Freywood castle.

They rode all morning and stopped halfway when the sun shone straight above their heads, walking around a bit to stretch their legs. Rory took out bread and tenderloin for lunch. After he finished eating, Jacoby rubbed his hands together and blew warm breath into them.

"Let me." She took his hands in hers, and it felt like he had dipped them into warm water. They stared at each other.

"More?" she asked. He nodded. She rubbed his long fingers and increased the heat. He raised her hands to his cheeks and closed his eyes. Rory thought about the night she saw his frozen body lying by the Eternal Flame.

"Thank you for getting me out of the darkness. I had forgotten what the sunshine felt like. I don't expect anything from you, either. I'm just very excited. I can't tell you how much."

He opened his green eyes. "The engineers of the Briar have already built a library, and if you decide to make a life there, I'm going to give it to you."

She looked wide-eyed and a little choked up. "Give it to me? The whole library?"

"Yes."

She shook her head. "How could I refuse?"

"Don't think about it now. You ready to mount up?"

They climbed onto Toby again and continued up the trail.

❧❦❧❦❧❦❧

As dusk began to settle in, the path opened up to a meadow. There was a thin strip of land cleared of snow in front of a small, brown castle. The sun and warmer temperatures had begun to melt the white blanket covering the stone building. Icicles dripped and fell from the edges. Four men pushed the large doors open, and they rode directly to a barn inside the gates.

A couple of stable hands, seemingly waiting on Jacoby, safely stowed the sled and Toby in a stall. Jacoby took the metal box out, and they proceeded to follow two guards, who held their bags, toward the king's main hall.

They paused outside before going in. Jacoby motioned for Rory to look at a long row of black rectangles mounted to a bracket that was stuck into the ground. A woman with a broom swept off the snow.

"They're called solar panels. They use the rays of the sun for power, which provides light and power inside the castle."

The lights mounted along the walls of the hallway amazed her. She could hear music playing, but it didn't sound anything like the few instruments she had heard at the Crossroads.

The guards took them up some stone steps to another bright hallway with multiple doors on each side.

One spoke to Jacoby. "The king has provided clean clothes in your rooms. He is hosting a party in the main hall and wants you to be the guest of honor for disposing of the dragons. We have prepared a feast as well. I will send for you in about half an hour."

The guard pointed to a door on the left, and Jacoby went in. He then opened the first door to the right and let Rory enter before closing it behind her. The garnet-colored walls had to be at least ten feet tall, and a red velvet canopy bed sat next to a gold, full-length mirror propped against the wall and a black dresser.

She had never seen herself all at once before. Her plain blue dress looked dirty from the long ride. A pair of slim black pants were folded on the bed, along with the softest black sweater and black wool socks. Black lace-up boots sat on the floor. She tried it all on and stood in front of the mirror. The outfit was so form-fitting, but very comfortable. Rory decided she wanted more pants. She noticed the exquisite stitching and craftsmanship of each item, the same as Jacoby's clothes.

There was a knock at her door, and a young woman's voice called out, "Can I come in, ma'am?"

Rory answered yes, and a girl around twenty years of age, dressed similarly to her, walked in. She brought more clothes, a nightgown, soaps, lotions, towels, and a hairbrush.

The girl introduced herself. "I'm Darby. Well, Princess Darby. The king is my father. Come in here with me."

She led Rory into a room off the bedroom. Snow-white tile covered every surface from floor to ceiling, and a counter held a washbasin. A large white tub stood in the middle of the room. Another gigantic mirror hung above the counter. Darby turned a brass knob on the basin, and water poured from the pipe.

Rory couldn't believe everything she was seeing.

Darby nodded toward the tub. "After the party, you can get a nice bath before bed. Can I braid your hair for the celebration?"

Rory nodded in agreement, feeling a little overwhelmed. She finally spoke. "Thank you. I can't wait to tell the king how much I appreciate his hospitality. There are so many things I have yet to experience in this world. I was wondering, how did you know I would be coming here with Jacoby?"

Darby looked puzzled. "Jake sent word three days ago on his communicator. I guess you've not seen one before. It's a ... device that lets you input messages, and they come through to another communicator."

All Rory could say was "oh."

She was taken aback by all of the inventions she had never even heard of, and she noted that Darby must know Jacoby, since she had called him Jake.

Darby finished Rory's long, golden braid. It looked a bit like basket weaving. Rory felt so beautiful looking at herself again in the mirror.

"You ready to eat and dance?"

"Dance?" Rory asked.

Darby pulled her along. "Come on!"

The music got louder the closer they got to the main hall. A huge crowd danced to the pulsating beat. Music boomed from large black boxes that were positioned on the walls every few feet. Red and blue lights glittered overhead. On the left side of the hall sat a long table filled with fruit, cheese, various kinds of meat, and sweets.

Darby pulled Rory into the crowd, and they began to dance.

Jacoby walked in with King Whitlow. His eyes immediately went to Rory's bright blond braid, bobbing up and down to the music. She looked so vibrant, enjoying the moment. Darby noticed Jacoby and ran to him with a hug.

"Hello, princess," he said, grinning.

Rory joined them, and Jacoby said, "Rory, I see you've met the princess. This is King Whitlow. He's going to show us the books tomorrow morning."

Rory gave a bow. "King Whitlow, I'm so honored to meet you and grateful for the opportunity to venture away from the middle of the mountain. There is so much yet to be seen. Thank you for the beautiful room and supplies."

He took her hand and kissed it, and she knew he could feel it was very hot.

"Are you feeling all right, dear? You feel very warm."

Rory glanced at Jacoby and quickly replied, "Oh yes, sir, I'm sure it's the dancing."

Darby chimed in. "Jake, let's get Rory some wine."

Rory refused the offer and asked, "Is there a balcony where I could step outside for a moment to cool off?"

Jacoby touched her arm and directed her through a door across the room. Rory gave off strong pulses into his palm as he joined her outside.

Rory insisted, "I don't want you to get cold. You stay. Dance. I'm fine, really."

He laughed. "I don't think I'll get cold if I'm near you." He took both of her hands in his and soothed her. "You seem nervous. Are you nervous?"

"You read me so well. Yes. I'm not sure about my sleeping arrangements. The bed is completely flammable. I almost thought about sleeping in the tub, but that seems silly. I may ask a favor of you. You don't have to say yes. Would you lie with me? Just ... lie next to me to sleep. As you can feel right now, when I'm very hot, I seem to give off extra heat, and for some reason, I have a reaction of vibrations with you. I'm sure if your arm was touching mine, you would sense it and could wake me up."

Jacoby's eyes narrowed in thought.

"No one would have to know. You could sneak in later and leave early if you are worried about your reputation."

He laughed at that. "My reputation? Why do you worry about my reputation? Darling, no one thinks a thing about who or how many people you sleep with these days. To tell you the truth, half the crowd at the party will be swapping partners by the end of the night. I would love to lie with you. You know what I mean." He laughed again.

"What about Darby? Does she expect you to spend the evening with her?"

He nodded. "Probably. Her father has offered her hand in marriage along with the books as my reward. I know it sounds absurd, but it's not an unusual occurrence. Kingdoms and colonies barter literally everything, even their children. When I don't show up to her chambers tonight, she will know I'm not accepting the offer." He had been rubbing his thumb across her knuckles.

Rory squeezed his hands. "Jake, you don't have to stay with me tonight if you need to go to her. I didn't come along with you to change your plans. I don't want to interfere with your life. I'm so very grateful to be here."

He shook his head. "I don't want to marry Darby. There are a lot of responsibilities I have to tend to when we get to the Briar. A new wife is not one of them just yet. Her father will understand."

Rory placed her hands to Jacoby's cheeks, pulled his head down, and kissed his forehead.

"Thank you. You should go back and join the party. I'm going to take a cool bath. I'll see you after."

She slipped back inside and went to her room.

The later it got, the more sensual the crowd became. The wine flowed, the music was intoxicating, and everyone seemed sweaty and aroused. Jacoby needed to leave the scene. He knew he was already going to have to show restraint sleeping with Rory. He left the celebration and went to his room to take a cold shower himself.

❄❄❄❄❄

Rory felt like a princess when she slipped the black silk gown over her head. She lathered her body in the lotion Princess Darby had brought, smelling of honeysuckle from head to toe.

It had to be around midnight. Rory sat at the dresser, brushing her squeaky-clean hair. She thoroughly enjoyed looking at herself in the mirror. It intrigued her to make note of her physical traits in such detail. The door opened, and Jacoby tiptoed inside. When he saw her awake, it startled him.

"Woman! Why are you still up? I was expecting to find you asleep." He did a twirl in front of her in his black silk pajama pants.

His bare chest caught her eye as he ran a hand down his abdomen. "Fancy, huh?" They laughed together.

"I know! I feel royal tonight. I bet you are used to all of this."

He hopped into bed and got under the covers. "I have to admit, the Briar has all of this and more. I can't wait for you to see."

He yawned and lay back on the red sheets. Two minutes later, he was silently asleep.

Rory put the brush down and climbed in next to Jacoby. She laid her arm next to his and fell asleep.

Jacoby's snoring woke Rory a short time later. She turned on her side facing away from him but couldn't block out the noise.

She whispered over her shoulder, "Jake! Jake, turn over. You're snoring too loud."

He grumbled and flipped his body toward her, throwing his long arm around her waist. He snuggled up behind her, enjoying her warmth. She wasn't sure what to do, but he was now silent. Not that she didn't love the intimacy she had been so long without. His chest pressed against her back comforted her, and she drifted back into slumber.

❊❊❊❊❊

Jacoby smelled honeysuckle before he even opened his eyes. He blinked, but the room was still dark. The sun was not up yet. He felt the silk gown against his skin and Rory's fingers intertwined with his. He didn't want to move. He nuzzled his nose into her hair and inhaled her scent.

She felt his movements and stretched her legs but held on to his hand.

Her voice quiet, she said, "Jake ... are you awake?"

He only replied with "mmm hmm." He didn't release her.

She asked, "You've been all around. Have you seen anyone like me, or even someone different, for that matter? Someone with abnormal abilities?"

He tightened his arm around her just a little. "I think so. What I mean is ... like you, I think they hide their abilities well. I think you will be surprised how diverse the world is. Have you decided to come to the Briar?"

She turned onto her back, sliding under his arm so that his hand still lay on her stomach. "Yes. I'm going to be honest. I'm scared. It's such a whirlwind."

He removed his hand from her tummy to gently tuck her hair behind her ear. "Rory, I won't let anyone hurt you. There are things you should know. I don't mean to frighten you, but as I mentioned before, humans aren't the only inhabitants of this Earth anymore. You were stowed away inside the mountain and it was safe, but you have no idea what the present time holds for you. It can be scary, but it's also full of wonder and opportunity for an amazing life. We have seen documents of the past. Some as far back as 2090. Even before that, the world's governments had what was called the 'Disclosure.' It was a declaration to the human race that we were not alone in the universe. These other beings are known as aliens, and they came here to Earth. There was a time when there were battles, seizures of smaller cities, and lots of casualties, both human and alien. Eventually, treaties were signed and efforts toward peace were made. There are even some humans and aliens who have settled in communities together. The aliens resemble humans and have hair and eyes like yours. Rory, I believe your father may have been of alien descent."

She slowly scooted to sit up in the bed and raised her hands to examine them. Light filtered through the drapes. She was in shock, but a sense of relief washed over her, knowing there may be an explanation for her condition.

"This is all so much to absorb. I understand some of what you're telling me, I just don't have words to express myself yet. Now I'm really scared," she said with a half laugh.

Jacoby rolled out of bed, went to the window, and looked outside.

He assured her, "Don't be scared. There's a lot more good in the world than bad. We're probably up before everyone else. I'm sure some stayed up all night. After surviving hard times, people tend to live lavishly and relish in the extravagant."

Rory tried not to stare at his bare torso. She was very sexually attracted to him, and he was her first intimate friend in years. She couldn't get attached to him. He was of some importance at the Briar and would soon be their leader. She reminded herself that she was only along for the ride, but she would cherish this time with him.

He came back to her and crawled under the sheets.

She giggled. "Are you chilly?"

He nodded, and she slid back down and put her warm feet on his ice-cold ones.

"Mmm."

"So, how far are we from the Briar?"

"Well, if we were traveling by horse, it would take three days."

She wondered what he meant.

"I have sent word for an airship to pick us up this afternoon. It's like a cruising ship with a gigantic balloon attached. It's filled with gas and floats through the sky. We will spend one night aboard and reach the Briar late tomorrow night. We will need to monitor you on the ship. The gas is very flammable. Don't worry," he assured when she knit her eyebrows together.

She said nervously, "If you say so. I think the cool bath helped a lot. I'm still eating my arrowroot too. Thank you for understanding my situation. You've gone out of your way to accommodate me. I'm excited about the books. Maybe I could set the library up for you. It could be a job. I feel I should repay you for everything. I'm also a pretty good healer. Nigel and Renfroe taught me a lot."

Jacoby smiled. "That sounds perfect. We should probably get dressed. We can go find the kitchen. I'm starving."

He kissed her forehead and went across the hall back to his room.

✤✤✤✤✤✤

The clothes supplied by the king were all the same. Black pants. Black sweater. Rory was glad. She thought she may never wear dresses again. She tied her hair back with the black ribbon Darby had secured her braid with the night before.

Princess Darby was coming up when they each stepped out of their rooms into the hallway. They said good morning as if it was the first time seeing one another since the party.

"Good! You're both up. I was going to take you down for breakfast."

She acted a little cold toward Jacoby, since he hadn't accepted the king's offer, so they followed her down in silence.

King Whitlow was already seated, and plates were set, ready to be eaten. There was more food than could be consumed. The king told them about the twelve crates full of dusty but intact books.

After eating, the four of them walked together to a large room that looked like an office with a few desks and chairs. The crates sat lined up against the wall.

Rory stepped over to one and asked, "May I?"

The king nodded. Jacoby pried off the dusty top, and she pulled out the first book she saw. The cover was pretty dirty, but the pages inside were pristine.

She flipped to the first page and read the date. "1944. This book is over a thousand years old! *Pride and Prejudice*. Can I keep it out, Jake, to take on the airship?"

He touched her elbow, seeing the adoration for the book in her eyes. "Of course." Then he spoke in a low tone only she could hear. "They're yours, Rory. Will you read it to me?"

She blushed and nodded yes. "Will the ship carry all of them? I know nothing about airships."

The king answered, "Yes. Toby will even have a hold. You'll be amazed."

Jacoby disappeared with the king to talk about politics. Rory proceeded back to her room to dust off her precious book and pack her things for their departure. She was still full of nervous energy, so she went to Jacoby's room and packed his things for him.

He walked in as she was finishing up. He grinned, happy to see her. The companionship made him feel like a different man. He loved her thoughtfulness.

❈❈❈❈❈

The Briar city center had a magnificent Art Deco style theater. Citizens performed a different play or concert every weekend. At the Briar there were plenty of women around, some whose jobs were to escort the colony's important council and military members to social functions. Jacoby was always accompanied by the same woman. Her name was Evelyn, but she went by Evie. She was tall and thin, with long jet-black hair. She was a well-known, brilliant actress, and beautiful, but very pampered. She and Jacoby had nothing in common personally, although they had been intimate, only to satisfy his physical needs. That was just the way of the world. Everyone knew what purpose the other served. Jacoby had a feeling it was all about to change for him as he looked down at Rory, who had just placed the last of his things in his bag, returning his smile. "Jake, I'm so excited. I packed early. I just couldn't help myself. I hope you don't mind."

He came closer. "No. not at all. You're very good at taking care of me. You don't have to, but thank you. I know you said you feel the need to repay me, but don't forget, you saved my life. I owe you everything. You will be taken care of at the Briar, and I want you to have fun with the library. Don't feel like you have to work off a debt to me."

He moved to stand behind her, placed his large hands on her shoulders, and began massaging them.

"How are you besides excited? I know it will be overwhelming."

She closed her eyes and melted in his hands. "Umm, this helps. Do you do this on the side?"

He laughed. "Only for you."

She reached up and put her hand on his. "I know things will be different when we arrive. You know my past. I want you to know how much I will treasure this short time with you. You will be the leader of the colony, but I consider you my friend. If you ever need to talk or find yourself in need of my warm feet, just ask."

They both laughed.

He turned her around to face himself. "You are the best friend I've had in a very long time. It's true, I'll be busy for a while, but ... we do have one more night before my responsibilities begin."

He bent his head down and pressed his lips to hers. It was a slow, sensual kiss that made both their hearts pound. His mouth lingered near hers, and she grabbed his waist, pulling him against herself as she took his mouth for another taste. She made his entire body tingle with electricity. They swayed backward, and when the back of her knees touched the bed, she sank down, pulling him on top. He kissed her neck, and she moaned.

Jacoby stopped all of a sudden and looked down at her. "I'm sorry. I don't want you to think I'm taking advantage of you."

Rory laughed. "Oh Jake. I think I'm a willing participant. I'm not innocent, you know."

"I know. I thoroughly enjoy kissing you. You make me feel like a teenager again."

He rolled off her and stared at the ceiling.

She sat up and straightened her sweater. "Why don't we take our things down? I want to thank the king again for everything."

He looked up at her and sighed. "Okay."

CHAPTER THREE

King Whitlow stood at the castle gates watching the airship slowly descend from the sky into the open meadow. A guard had Toby ready to board. They thanked King Whitlow and continued toward the clearing.

As they walked through the gates, Rory slowed down to take it all in. The airship was beautiful. The balloon was white and shiny. A deck adorned the top with an intricately carved wood railing all the way around. Two rows of stained glass windows lined the sides.

Jacoby put his arm around her shoulder and pointed to the huge front window. "Up there, that's the captain's room. He controls the whole ship. I'll show you. And ... we will be rooming in the back, far away from the fuel tanks."

The big boat floated down gently, and crew members threw ropes down to men on the ground. They staked them down temporarily to keep it steady. Jacoby and Rory walked up a plank and into the doorway.

The inside was made up entirely of dark mahogany wood. Red, ornate rugs covered the floors. Paintings of hunting dogs and horses framed in gold hung on the walls. Two men dressed in brown uniforms took their belongings and led them down a hallway that seemed to go on forever.

Finally, they stopped at the last door on the left. Rory and Jacoby followed them into the cozy room. It resembled the front entrance—mostly mahogany—and had a black iron bed covered with dark blue blankets and four puffy pillows. The men sat the bags down beside a tall wooden dresser. Jacoby shook their hands and thanked them on their way out.

He turned to her, motioning around the room. "So, it's not the royal quarters, but pretty nice, right? Captain Barton takes a lot of pride in his ship."

Rory laughed. "It's lovely. A dry, clean room is all I ask for. I'm easy to please."

Jacoby took her hand in his and pulled her out of the room back down the long hallway. Halfway, he took them up a set of stairs that led to the deck. There were women dressed like maids scurrying around, looking very busy. Everyone aboard would nod to Jacoby and call him sir. They stepped up to the rail and watched the crew wind up the ropes that had been holding the ship in place. One woman brought a long black cape to Jacoby and placed it over his shoulders. He closed the clasp in the front. Now he certainly looked like a leader.

He leaned down and whispered in her ear, "This is all formality. High ranks of the military wear these. It's not my ideal attire."

She giggled. "It's so very regal. Seriously though, Jake, it suits you. I should probably call you ... what? I mean, I need to be respectful like everyone else."

He shook his head. "Yes. I guess you should. My title is major general."

She smiled. "Very authoritative." She whispered to him, "I find the cape very attractive." She sounded naughty when she said it, and it took him by surprise.

The ship soared upward, and they waved goodbye to Darby and King Whitlow.

"I want to show you the flight room."

They stayed on the deck and walked straight toward the front of the ship. There was a large cabin with huge, clear windows on every side. They went in to meet the captain. It smelled of pipe tobacco, and all sorts of maps lay on a table that ran the length of the room. A beautiful globe stood beside the steering wheel. The dashboard with all sorts of buttons looked high tech, unlike a traditional ship's helm.

Jacoby heartily shook the captain's hand. "So good to see you, my friend. I have quite a tale to tell about my quest. Rory, Captain Quinn Barton. Quinn, this is Rory Larken. She's going to be staying at the Briar. She will set up the library and can probably teach our healers a thing or two."

"It's my pleasure to meet you, captain. Major General Garrick is being too kind. Thank you for providing our transportation."

Quinn lifted her hand and kissed it. He was a very handsome, tall, lean man with short, light brown, curly hair and piercing blue eyes. He looked to be about her age.

"I look forward to dining together and hearing all about you, Ms. Larken."

She nodded in agreement and looked at Jacoby, whose mouth was in a straight line. He didn't look too happy about Quinn flirting with her. Quinn wasn't used to Jacoby caring. Quinn flirted with every beautiful woman.

Jacoby's bright mood darkened a bit. "We will join you in the galley shortly after we get a chance to change."

✤✤✤✤✤✤

As they walked back to their room, Jacoby didn't say a word. He took off the cape and sat on the edge of the bed in silence while Rory unpacked.

He finally spoke. "There are a few dresses in the closet. It's expected that a woman wears a dress to dinner. I'll turn around while you get ready."

He walked over to the pale, rose window and watched the clouds pass by.

Every dress was black. She pulled out the only one that looked to be her size. It had a long skirt but dipped in an extremely low V in the front and back. Once in it, she had never felt so exposed. She was definitely not used to popular fashion.

She spoke to him while she made sure her breasts were covered. "Is something wrong? What's going on in that head of yours?"

He answered in a deep voice. "To be honest, I got jealous. I'm not sure I've ever been jealous before. Also, I'm just thinking ... we only have tonight and tomorrow left. After I get you settled, I may not see you as much for a while. I just don't know."

She came up behind him, slid her arms around his waist, and pressed her cheek against his back. "It's okay, Jake. Don't worry about my feelings. It's flattering that you were jealous over me. We could lounge in bed all day tomorrow and I can read my book to you."

Rory knew her vibrations around his body soothed his anxiousness.

He took a few deep breaths to relax. "I would love it if you read to me. Now, let me see this dress."

He turned around to face her and looked her up and down with such desire. "Rory. I ... you're making it hard for me."

She leaned up on her tiptoes and planted a short kiss on his mouth. Her face close to his, she said, "Let's just enjoy our time together. Oh, and you'll have to tell me if a body part slips out of this tiny top."

They both laughed, and he assured her he would.

He held her hand as they walked into the galley, where he stopped with a jolt, which jerked Rory back a little bit. He let go of her and apologized.

Quinn had his back to them, standing at the carved wood bar with a gorgeous woman. He turned, smiled, and glided over to Rory. He kissed her hand again and didn't let go. It was obvious he was assessing the fit of her dress.

"Ms. Larken, you are a vision. I must thank the major general again for bringing you to us."

She had a weird feeling, like he expected something from her. He let go of her hand, and Jacoby moved to stand right at his side.

He growled into Quinn's ear, "I don't believe you brought Evie with you. Why would you do that? I'm really not in the mood."

Quinn smiled slyly. "Sir, my intentions were good, I assure you. I thought perhaps you might be in need of her services."

Rory knew exactly what he was getting at.

Jacoby ran his hand through his hair and sighed heavily. "Well, perhaps *you* can use her services tonight."

He grabbed Rory's hand again and took her to sit at a large round table covered with a fancy white cloth. One of the women she had seen earlier on the deck brought wine and cheese to the table and lit the tapered white candle that stood in the middle. Quinn whispered into Evie's ear, and they joined Jacoby and Rory at the table.

Evie ate her food in silence and didn't even look at Jacoby. Quinn asked Rory to tell him about herself. She spoke of the Crossroads and being an innkeeper, of her sheltered, meager life. "I'll let the major general tell you how I came to be here."

Jacoby cleared his throat. "Rory saved my life."

She looked at him nervously, afraid he would expose her ability, but his eyes told her she could trust him.

"I disposed of the dragons but pressed my luck with the weather. I don't know what possessed me to ride into the night while a blizzard was brewing, but I did. Toby didn't give up. He's lucky he didn't freeze. He rode toward the closest source of heat, I think. I only remember the warmth of a fire and lying in Rory's lap, being forced to drink ale that warmed me from the inside. Rory thawed me out by the flames and tucked me into a warm bed. She stayed with me all night, monitoring me. I do remember people speaking around me, talking about my slow heart rate and shallow breathing. Rory brought me through. I'm giving her the library as a small thanks for my life."

Evie finally spoke up. "So, Rory's a hero. She brought our soon-to-be governor back to us. We are all in your debt." She surprised Rory with her kind words.

Rory smiled. "I did what any decent person would do. I'm so thankful to be here. There is much I need to learn about the world."

Quinn added, "My dear, I will take you to the theater soon. Evie is the most loved actress in the colony. She can get us front-row seats."

Jacoby felt jealous again, but he wanted Rory to experience everything the Briar had to offer and didn't know when he would be able to socialize. The only problem with Quinn was he had a hard time keeping his hands to himself.

Rory yawned, and Jacoby motioned to a server. He asked for dessert and wine to go.

With Quinn and Evie watching, he grabbed Rory's hand. "I'm pretty beat myself. We are going to retire early. I'm going to be working on some city plans in my room all day tomorrow, so we will see you when we reach the Briar."

The two were surprised at even the smallest public affection Jacoby was showing toward Rory.

Quinn stood when they did to bid them good night. After they left, Evie asked Quinn, "Want some company tonight?"

❊❊❊❊❊❊

When they were back in their room, Rory could tell Jacoby was relieved dinner was over. He unbuttoned his shirt and lay on the bed.

"Sorry if that was a little awkward. Quinn, well ... Quinn loves women. Evie usually accompanies me to events. The unmarried officials never attend functions alone. It's just the way they do it in our colony. Evie has spent many nights with me, but to tell you the truth, I don't really know much about her."

Rory walked to the closet. "You don't owe me any explanation. She's lovely. I would like to see the theater."

He sighed. "I only told you because I want you to know the way things work at the Briar. I want to make it as easy as I can for you to get acclimated, since I won't be around for a while. I also told you because I have a deep affection for you. I care about what you think of me."

Rory undressed in front of Jacoby and put on her long silk gown, then walked over to the bed and took it upon herself to remove his boots. She sat them by the door and retrieved his pajama pants from the dresser.

She laid them beside him. "I'm going across the hall to the washroom. Be right back."

When she returned, she found Jacoby sitting beside the tray of dark wine and dessert. He patted the bed for her to join him, so she crawled up next to him. His long legs hung off the edge of the bed. He was propped up on one arm, bare-chested and looking better than dessert. She picked up the full glass of wine and drank it down in one gulp.

Jacoby started to laugh and raised his thick, dark eyebrows, amused. "This is all stressing you out tremendously, is it?"

She laughed with him. "A little. I wouldn't trade it for anything, though."

After eating the chocolate mousse with decadent raspberry filling, Rory placed the tray on the dresser. She opened a drawer, took out her book, and stretched out across the bed on her stomach.

"Do you want me to start it tonight? You look as though you'll be asleep after the first sentence."

He laughed a little. "Sure. I think you're right, though." Jacoby slid up next to her. He reached out and tilted her chin so that they were staring into each other's eyes. "Can I kiss you again?"

Rory put the book on her pillow and leaned nearer, whispering, "Please."

The first kiss was sweet and soft. He rolled onto his back and pulled her on top of his long body. They tasted each other more passionately now. His hands spanned her back, pressing her against his chest. She placed little kisses down his jawline to his neck. It pained him to release her from his embrace. Rory, for her part, didn't want to detach from Jacoby.

She raised her head. "I sure will miss you when I don't see you every day."

He gave her a sweet peck on her lips and agreed. "One day. One day, I'll come back to you. I'll always come back to you. You're like my lucky talisman. When I'm near you I feel like my complete self, and my stress fades away."

She shook her head. "We make quite the pair, don't we? I'm going to read to you. I'll stop when you go to sleep."

His arms loosened, and she slid off to lie next to him, pulling the rich blue blankets down. They curled up underneath. She propped the book up on her knees, and it automatically opened to the very middle. There she found a yellowed newspaper clipping. The headline read "Beware the dragons! They should not be trusted." The photo under the title was not of a dragon. The male looked human, but not quite. The picture was black and white, but she could tell he had blonde or white hair, like hers. The eyes almost looked silver. There was a drawing beside the photo of a palm holding a flame. The article was cut off. Rory was astounded. She flipped the paper over but saw no date.

Jacoby looked up at her, waiting for her to read. "Rory? What is it?"

She felt too many things. She managed to whisper, "Jacoby, you didn't kill a dragon like I understand a dragon to be, did you?"

He didn't answer. She continued, louder. "It was an alien like you told me about. And you think I'm a descendant of aliens, so why am I here? What do you want from me? Are you taking me back as a prize? Why would you kill them?"

He stumbled over his words. "Rory, listen, don't jump to conclusions. Let me try to give you answers. I truly don't have all the answers you seek, but I want to be honest with you, I swear."

Tears flowed from the hurt at the thought of him deceiving her. Sweat beaded up on her body, and her temperature rose rapidly. With a quickness, she jumped out of the bed and ran across the hall to the washroom. She jerked the cold-water knob on the bathtub and pulled her gown off. The door stood open.

Jacoby followed close behind, worried she might burn up. He found her sitting in the tub panting. He didn't talk. He found a washcloth and began squeezing cool water over her shoulders and back. She closed her eyes and dried her hot tears. Her breathing slowed to normal.

She is perfect, he thought. He didn't care that she was part alien. She was very human to him.

He finally spoke in a soothing, deep voice. "I want you to trust me. I have excellent reasons why. I ... I would die before I hurt you, or let anyone hurt you, my sweet Rory. Please, don't hate me. I couldn't bear it."

He washed her face with the cool water. She glanced up at him, looking like a scared animal. He lowered his head to touch hers. She wrapped her arms around his neck and stood up, dripping. He hugged her close. He pulled back only to get her covered with a towel and then scooped her up to carry her back to their room.

Rory mumbled into his chest, "I'm sorry I'm such a mess." The episode took a lot of energy out of her. He sat her on a tufted stool beside the bed and gave her a piece of arrowroot from her bag.

"I'm going to get your gown."

He was back in a second and laid it on the bed before picking up the book and clipping that were on the floor. "I promise I won't hide anything from you ever again. I believe you are a part of this alien race we call dragons, because of their ability to control fire and the violent nature of their attacks. When they first arrived, they laid waste to many cities by burning them to the ground. Their weapons are similar to ours but more advanced. Many humans and livestock died, and they used up the viable crops. They took a lot of the women captive, enslaving them and sexually abusing them. I'm afraid that's what happened to your mother. I have a feeling she escaped when the humans took back some of the cities but was already pregnant with you."

"My father was a general in the army that defeated most of them. A lot of the high-ranking dragons ran off in small groups to remote locations and survived. I spent my twenties as a bounty hunter solely focused on extinguishing as many as I could. When the army found human women and children, they were sent to special protected colonies. We call the offspring biraces, or halves. I have encountered some of the children who have grown up and interacted with them. Most can control fire but would not show me out of fear. None of them ever caused a physical reaction in me the way you do. I don't even have to touch you and I feel you on my skin. It's like your being is flowing through me. You calm me at a level I'll never understand."

She finished the arrowroot and sat staring at him.

He desperately croaked out, "Rory, say something, please."

She reached out her hand to him. He slowly slid his palm against hers and closed his eyes. He inhaled a long, deep breath and exhaled.

"I believe you, Jake. There are too many mysteries in this universe for me to grasp, but somehow, I know deep down that it's going to be okay. Like Nigel told me, I was meant for more in this life."

44

He opened his eyes to look at her beautiful face and smiled. "When I started on my journey, I never could have imagined finding you. We should get you back into your gown. You need your rest. We will have all day tomorrow to spend however we like."

He walked around to his side of the bed and hopped in. Rory slid the gown over her head and pulled the towel out from under it. She retrieved her lotion before getting in on her side.

She sighed, and felt lighter. "I love this fragrance. I hope you have some like it at the Briar," Rory said as she covered her arms and legs.

Jacoby enjoyed the smell as well. "Oh yes. I'm sure we can make it if we don't already have it. We have real scientists. They can make all sorts of things."

Pulling the covers up to her waist and scooting over to him, she laid her arm over his chest, and he put his arm around her so that she could rest her head by the crook of his neck.

She made a purring sound. "Is this all right?"

"Darling, there's no place I'd rather be," he said sweetly. Then he sighed. "This night. This last night alone with you is a double-edged sword. I despise the darkness because I know when the sun rises everything will change."

❊❊❊❊❊

Before first light, Rory woke up. Her body was sprawled over Jacoby like a sheepskin. He was still in deep sleep, so she gingerly rolled off him, got out of bed, and went across the hall to use the washroom.

When she opened the door, a tall, bare-chested man with disheveled curls and sleepy eyes stood as still as a brick wall and smiled when he saw her. Quinn surprised her, and she halted in the doorway.

He came up only inches away from her, smelling of stale ale. "Ms. Rory. Good morning, beautiful." Bold fingers reached out and played with the ends of her hair, very nearly touching her breast.

"I hated seeing you retire so early last night. Would you like to join me for a bath?" He brazenly touched the strap of her gown, and it fell off her shoulder.

She quickly slid it back into place. "No thank you, captain. I took my bath last night."

Still, he didn't move. There was nowhere to go, and he was very obviously aroused. Her heart beat faster. After a few seconds, he relented and stepped aside.

"Suit yourself, darling."

Rory darted into her room, slamming the door behind her. She leaned against it, trying not to hyper-ventilate. Jacoby had woken up when the door banged shut. He flipped on the lamp and immediately saw the panic on her face.

He appeared next to her in a flash. "Are you over-heating? What's wrong?" He grabbed her arms, but they weren't hot. He pulled her against his chest.

She felt safe now in Jacoby's arms. "Quinn just appeared out of nowhere in the hallway. He ... he tried to touch me and suggested I join him for a bath. His words didn't upset me so much, but he seemed drunk and I'm not sure what he's capable of—"

Jacoby cut her off in anger. "You should have called out for me. I was right here. I'll kill him ..."

She put her hand over his heart, calming him. "It's okay. I refused, and he backed off. I would have made a scene if he persisted. I won't go anywhere without telling you."

Her touch put him at ease. His eyes went heavy. "Rory, I wish I could stake my claim on you. No one would dare bother you if you were mine. I'm so jealous when I think of you belonging to another."

She wanted to tell him to stake his claim. Her heart was all his, but she couldn't share her want for him. He was too important. She kept quiet.

He whispered, "Maybe ... later ..."

Rory put her fingers on his lips to hush his words. He held her tight and kissed the top of her head. His stomach growled, and they laughed.

He let her go, took his communicator from the dresser drawer, and spoke into the black circle that resembled a futuristic pocket watch.

"Ordered room service. Have you ever had waffles? They are sinful."

She shook her head no and laughed again. "I'm starving."

She meandered over to the window. The colored glass made everything pink. Jacoby changed into gray, uniform-style pants and a black T-shirt. He was so well built and looked good in anything. Rory admired his beautiful, long arms and large hands. She followed suit and put on her fitted black pants. She was thankful King Whitlow had sent her with an endless supply of gray, short-sleeved tops, since she needed to keep cool.

A hard knock on the door signaled the arrival of breakfast, and Jacoby took the brass cart from the kitchen help. There were two silver dishes and fresh milk. Rory lifted the shiny domes to reveal golden waffles, muffins, butter, and cups of warm liquid the color of amber. It smelled heavenly, not sinful.

After eating, Rory made up the bed while Jacoby went to the washroom to clean up. Her thoughts battled like a game of tug-of-war. She desired Jake like no other and had a feeling that if she offered herself, he wouldn't refuse. That's the side her body pulled for, but her brain and heart knew better. Rory was unsure of what the future held. Her instincts told her not to give him that precious intimacy yet.

As she packed her belongings, she looked inside the ancient book again to make sure the newspaper article was safe before she tucked it into her bag.

Jacoby returned dressed, looking like a common colony dweller. She glanced at his bare feet, which surprisingly turned her on. An image of two bodies tangled together played out in her mind, and she had to refocus. She sat at the dresser to pull back her hair. Jake sat on the bed and tugged on his socks and boots.

"I noticed lots of maps on the captain's desk. Can I see them? It might give me an idea of where I'm going to be living. Sometimes I feel like a new fawn first learning of her surroundings."

Jacoby smiled. "Of course. It isn't your fault, you know. Living in a secluded area."

She sighed. "I know, but it's a little frustrating. If you hadn't shown up, I'd be doing laundry for the rest of my days."

He rose and came to stand behind her. Both looked at their reflections in the mirror. "Now look at you." He touched her hair—he couldn't resist—then drew his hand back.

"Quinn will be there. Will you be all right?"

"Yes," she replied firmly.

❖❖❖❖❖

Quinn looked surprised to see Rory walk through the door with Jacoby. He seemed a little uncomfortable. He had to know she had told Jake about what had happened.

He nodded. "Jake, ah, major general. Can I have a word with Ms. Larken alone for just a moment?"

Jake looked at Rory, his mouth set in a line of concern. She focused on Quinn. "Sure."

Jacoby spoke to Quinn directly. "I'll be back in a bit. Show Ms. Larken your maps. She's interested in gaining a bit of knowledge about her world." He stepped out and closed the door behind him.

Quinn didn't come near, but looked sincerely into her eyes. "Rory ... Ms. Larken ..."

A few seconds passed between them.

"I'm dreadfully sorry for my behavior. I, um, I haven't always been very respectful toward women. I'm just being brutally honest." His hand went to his heart.

Rory could hardly believe his sincerity. "Go on."

He apprehensively eased closer.

"You inspire me to be better. To do better. I was surprised Jake didn't hunt me down after what I said to you. A little too much to drink on my part. I have thought about it all morning, and I deeply regret it. I'm asking for your forgiveness." He held out a friendly hand. She took it, and he held on, escorting her to the desk, then let go and placed a long finger on the closest map.

"This is the Briar."

The colony appeared large, but not sprawling, and very secure. A fortified fence of solid brick surrounded the city. It contained everything a city needed to flourish: plenty of housing units and some homesteads alongside farming land on the outskirts of the city center, which consisted of the theater, some restaurants, the new library, a mercantile, and the Central Military Office. A small park sat between riding stables and a lake. They would travel over the River of Light and arrive at a highly guarded intake facility attached to the Central Military Office.

Rory enjoyed her time with Quinn, and seeing the maps amplified her excitement about beginning a new life. She adored the globe, and Quinn promised to put one in the library. He had made such a turnaround from just hours ago. Rory felt they might be good friends in time.

Jacoby entered the cabin to the sound of laughter. The pair seemed to be getting along perfectly, and jealousy rose in him. The captain, always a charmer, had worked his magic once again.

"We should reach the Briar in a couple of hours. Our things are ready to disembark. Let's get lunch. The council will probably send me straight to the Central

Military Office, and I want to spend a few minutes with you alone," Jacoby ordered, pulling Rory toward the door.

Quinn followed. "Oh, I'll make sure Ms. Larken makes it safely to her apartment."

Jacoby turned to him, speaking in a low voice. "Did you apologize?"

He firmly replied, looking past Jacoby. "Yes, sir. Ms. Rory can place her full trust in me, sir." A flash glinted in his eyes, and it stirred something inside her.

Jacoby noticed the exchange and quickly escorted her out of the room. He kept hold of her hand as they made the walk back to eat. When they were alone again, she sat him down on the edge of the bed. His annoyance permeated the room. She pulled his chin up, so that he concentrated on her face.

"Calm yourself. You have a lot going on." She ran her hands through his hair, and he closed his eyes. Her energy traveled from his scalp down to his toes. Arousal warmed the space between them as he wrapped his arms around her waist and buried his face in her abdomen. She held on, treasuring the moment.

A man in uniform delivered lunch and draped a freshly cleaned black cape over the bed, then left with their bags as they enjoyed mouthwatering roast beef.

With a full belly, Jacoby covered the trays and undressed to don his proper uniform. Rory stared out of the window. The airship passed over a body of water, which she recognized as the River of Light from the map. There were big, beautiful boats with masts in every color, all floating toward the city port at the Intake Center.

Jacoby stood close beside her. "You nervous? Want some arrowroot?" He offered it from his wide palm.

"Sure." She took it and held his hand. "How are you?"

He sighed and smiled. "I will be fine. You know I'm not happy about being apart from you. I will be busy tonight, but after my morning meeting, I want to take you to lunch and the library if I can. I will send a ride to pick you up. It is right across from my office in the CMO."

Rory smiled back.

"I'm so excited, Jake. Thank you so much for everything."

Her joy appeared to ease him. "Captain Barton will meet us at the loading port. He will accompany you after we enter the city."

His eyes darkened and pupils dilated. "Rory ..." He leaned in, smelled her scent, and caressed her cheek, placing his mouth on hers.

Electricity coursed between them as his tongue played around her mouth. The steady beat of his heart drummed against her palms. His hands fit against the curve of her back, and their blood burned together. She moaned, and he reluctantly loosened his hold on her.

Still forehead to forehead and breathing hard, she panted, "Oh, Jake. I'm glad I ate that arrowroot."

They laughed, took some deep breaths, and straightened their clothes. Rory picked up the long cape with a swish and placed it over the major general's shoulders. He closed the clasp, then turned and grabbed her close for one more embrace.

CHAPTER FOUR

R ory stood by Jacoby's side as they waited outside the intake facility. Her hand reached under the edge of his cape to touch his elbow, and she slid her palm in position to rest on his forearm. He immediately took in a slow breath and released it, feeling her soothing touch. No one else would notice, but she watched his face relax under her calming vibrations. The straight line of his mouth curved up at the corner.

Rory felt nostalgic already, knowing this precious shared intimacy might be the last physical contact she would experience for an indeterminate amount of time. He may be whisked away from her without a second glance. What if the council kept him too busy? She was unsure if she could bear it. Rory calmed herself, blocked the negativity, and reminded herself who the major general was at the Briar. He was not the same Jake she knew.

Captain Barton appeared behind them as the bolts in the large door clicked to the unlock position. Jacoby turned to Rory, taking both her hands in his and quickly kissing them. Letting go, he stepped forward, straightening his posture. He looked very much like a leader. Quinn moved to her side, offering a genuine smile. He mouthed the words "it's okay" and winked.

She expected paved streets and tall buildings, but the chamber did not lead to the outside at all. A brightly lit, wide, rectangular hall with high ceilings was their

53

next stop. The Intake Center was larger than she had imagined.

A guard took Jacoby through a silver door behind a long desk, where Captain Barton motioned for her to join him. A girl with a notebook and pen took her name down. To Rory's surprise, the girl, whose nameplate read Jimena, looked very similar to herself. Silvery eyes and bright blonde hair must be defining characteristics of her kind.

Jimena looked her up and down. "The major general has vouched for your character and physical well-being. It is usually protocol to direct you to the Health Center, but your appointment is tomorrow morning. We have orders for Captain Barton to escort you to your apartment this evening. Welcome, and get some rest, Ms. Larken."

"Thank you, Jimena. Ms. Larken." Quinn offered his arm.

She took it, and they made their way down the corridor. She recognized the symbol of a red cross on one door—that would be an infirmary. Other doors held supplies and food as marked. Everyone who passed moved aside and nodded to Quinn. A banner reading "Welcome Home, Major General" hung over the double doors leading outside. The sun had already set. Streetlights lined gray sidewalks. Buildings of the same color soared toward the sky and glittered with lit windows.

Quinn paused so she could take it all in. He watched her eyes absorbing her surroundings, then gave her hand a small squeeze. "What do you think, Ms. Larken?"

She looked at his smiling face, and it calmed her nerves. He seemed excited to be able to have this experience with her.

Take a deep breath, she told herself, *and let it out*. "I can do this, right?"

"Yes. And I'm going to be right here any time you need anything. I thought we could walk a bit. Your apartment isn't that far, and I actually live in the same building."

"Does everyone live in large buildings together?"

"Most do. There are farms and a couple of housing communities on the outskirts of the city like you saw on the map. The location I showed you that said Crop Community. We have farmers who grow food and raise animals. Families with children live in the housing communities, and they help out on the farms."

"I haven't seen many children, even around Freywood. Is that because of the wars Jacoby spoke of?"

"I imagine so. Raising a family isn't a priority when you're in survival mode. We are only recently feeling safe enough to settle down, build a new world, if you will."

"Do you want children, captain?"

Quinn hadn't thought much about the subject. No one had ever asked. "I'm not sure yet, I guess. I've never seen myself as much of a father figure. I'll be honest, Rory. My past actions haven't proven to be those of a family man. The Briar is working on growing the population. That's a whole other story. Ah, here we are."

The modern building stood ten stories high. Rory counted them. Quinn let go of her hand when the frosted glass door opened on its own, and they entered a spacious foyer. On the left, brass boxes labeled with each apartment number lined the wall.

"These are for any post you might receive. The council sends out important memos or letters, and the theater sends out schedules for plays, music, and movies."

They stepped into an elevator, and Quinn showed Rory the rail on the inside. "Hold on. It moves pretty fast."

It zoomed upward, and she swayed and laughed as it stopped on the tenth floor.

Next was a lengthy, crisp white hallway with royal blue carpet.

"I'd like to take you to the theater soon. You'll love it."

Rory hadn't talked much. She listened to Quinn but felt too tired to ask questions. They came to apartment 105.

"And here's your place. I'm in 104. As promised, I'm close if you need me."

"I appreciate that, Captain Barton. Wow."

Her eyes flitted around the room. A small, modern kitchen took up most of the entry. Every surface was silver, and the walls white. The floors were light wood planking, and the windows displayed a gorgeous lake view. The gray seating appeared plush and comfortable.

Quinn took her bag to another room and returned. "Please call me Quinn."

Rory was tired, and he led her to the bedroom, where he had left her bag.

"You, Ms. Larken, need sleep. Uh, Rory, there is arrowroot in the cabinets, and your bedding is flame retardant." He went to the bedside table, took a communicator from the drawer, and set it on top.

She heard everything he said, but her attention was on the beautiful white bed; she longed to fold herself into the blankets.

"Press the blue button if you need me. The red is for an emergency, and yellow is for a central operator who can connect you with anyone you wish. The leaders don't allow the major general to be programmed in, but you can request him through the operator. We can talk more tomorrow after you rest. Good night, Ms. Larken."

He slipped out before she could thank him. Rory threw herself onto the bed, not even changing clothes, and went fast to sleep.

❊❊❊❊❊❊

The communicator woke Rory with four very loud, obnoxious beeps. She blinked and sat up. She had

56

never slept so well in her life. She shuffled to the bathroom and figured out how the shower worked after several attempts. It was her first one, and the hot water beating down over her felt like hot, steamy heaven. She towel-dried her hair, pulled it back, dressed, and went in search of fresh milk in the cold box, which also offered the most delicious fruit. Having everything on hand was delightful.

The communicator beeped again from the bedroom but didn't stop this time. She ran to pick it up and pressed the talk button. "Hello?"

Quinn's familiar voice came through. "Morning, Ms. Larken. Did you sleep well?"

"Yes. Too well, thank you."

"A car arrives in a few minutes. Do you need anything? Remember how to get back to the lobby?"

"I'll be fine. I'm ready. I will head down now."

"Listen, I'm betting the major general will be quite busy. Can I pick you up at the Health Center? We can stop by Jacoby's office if you want and get some lunch."

"Oh, yes. That would be nice. Thank you, Quinn."

The car was such a quick way to travel. Another first. More halves, like her, worked inside the medical center. One, a nurse with long blonde hair and silvery eyes, led her to a private room, where she handed Rory a flimsy gown to put on.

She smiled warmly. "The doctor will be in shortly."

The doctor who entered was a middle-aged, exotic-looking woman, and Rory let out a sigh of relief.

She held out a hand. "Hello, I'm Dr. Mora Lang. We are glad you are here. We have a healthy population of halves here, and you should settle in easily."

Her smile put Rory at ease. The doctor asked all sorts of questions, from what she knew about her parents to her sexual history. A very thorough physical exam followed, and blood was taken. Dr. Lang asked her to re-dress and wait a few minutes. When she returned, she closed the door behind her.

"Rory, you are very healthy. You control your abilities well. Better than anyone I've examined. The biraces, or halves, as we call them, like you are required to receive a specially formulated drug we have created here at the Briar. It suppresses the response to stressful stimuli, keeping the body temperature stabilized."

Rory glanced down. "That would be wonderful. It's been very isolating, worrying if I will overheat and cause a catastrophe."

Dr. Lang smiled. "I'm happy to help you with that. There's something else we should talk about. The fact that you were married over a year and sexually active without getting pregnant suggests you are unable. I believe the explanation is the simple fact that your body has never been regulated. You reported being very much above normal human body temperature levels at many points during your life. I believe that has caused your womb to become sterile."

The news did not come as a shock. Rory knew she should have been with child before now. "I understand completely, doctor."

Mora nodded. "We will start your vaccine today, and you will return once a month from now on. I'll have my nurse bring it in and then you can be on your way. Please call or come back here any time you need anything."

"Yes, of course. Thank you so much, Dr. Lang."

The same nurse from earlier brought in the shot. "Hello, Ms. Larken. I'm Alandriel. This will sting for a second, but we halves are so happy to have it. Do you have any questions?"

"Please, call me Rory. I am looking to find a few friends here. I would love to hear more about our kind."

"I have a break coming up. If you'd like, we can talk more, and I can show you around the center."

They met in the lobby of the building, which simulated an atrium with live plants and a water feature that produced a peaceful atmosphere. Alandriel was so easy-going, and Rory felt like she was meant to be at the Briar.

"I have a few close friends. Humans and halves. I heard the major general brought you here. Was he nice to you? No one seems to know much about him except that he is a good leader and will be the governor soon. I think he's a recluse. Every time I see him in public, his face is stern and a bit angry looking. He should smile more. He's so handsome."

Rory smirked. She knew a very different side of Jacoby. "He was a perfect gentleman. I aided him in a very important mission, and he gave me the library."

Alandriel's eyes lit up. "The new library? Oh, I can't wait for it to open. He gave it to you? It must have been super important."

Rory changed the subject. "So, I know a lot about treating illness. I was hoping to volunteer somewhere in the medical center."

"Oh, yes. Our troops still participate in small battles here and there. The infirmary always needs extra hands. Do you know about wounds?"

"Yes. That's perfect. After the library is ready, I'll have plenty of time. How long have you been here?"

"Since before I can remember. My mother is human. She lives here but is too old to conceive, so she works out on the farms. She's used to that life anyway."

"What does conceiving have to do with it?"

"During the two-year conflict, a lot of the human race was wiped out. Less than half of the previous population survived. The council has a program in place with the desired outcome of repopulating pure humans." She whispered, "They need to outnumber us."

"So ... exactly how are they accomplishing this?"

"Young, healthy women are having children with the strongest, most respected men."

"The major general too? He has children?"

"It's possible, although he has been gone a lot on special missions. It's nothing personal. It is all science.

The kids are raised by nannies on the outskirts of the city."

Rory remembered Quinn talking about growing the population, and that he was supposed to meet her soon. He arrived at the front desk just as he had in her thoughts.

Rory turned to Alandriel. "Thank you so much. We will talk again soon?"

"For sure! We can go shopping and see more of the city."

"It's a date."

Quinn looked handsome out of his flight team uniform. He wore blue slacks and a white button-down shirt that fit just right. His face beamed, and he took her hand.

"Rory, so good to see you. Did your appointment go well?" They walked out to the sidewalk and continued toward the library.

"Yes. I'm excited about the vaccine. It takes an immense amount of stress away, so I can focus on other things and enjoy myself. Thank you for looking after me. I'm sure you have things to keep you busy."

"Well, the military is constantly aware of everything going on outside of the city. My responsibilities are on hold until a threat is present. I have all the time in the world at the moment, and I hope you will allow me to spend some of it with you."

Two long black cars sat in front of the library. Armed men in uniform stood on each side of the door.

"Looks like the major general is here."

Once they entered, they saw Jacoby, who directed his words toward Quinn. "Come back in an hour, please."

Quinn looked surprised to be dismissed but obliged.

When they were alone, Jacoby grinned as he made his way to Rory and encircled her in a strong embrace.

"God, I needed to see you. To feel you around me. A full day has barely passed, but I missed you. Has Quinn behaved? How was your appointment this morning?"

He pulled back a bit, and she looked up at him.

"He's been a gentleman, and everyone at the medical center was so welcoming. I met a new friend. A half like me. We are going to get together soon. Dr. Lang gave me a vaccine I'm sure you already know about."

He still held her hands. "Of course. That's one thing less you have to worry about. I still feel your energy. I'm happy I still feel you. You calm me so."

Rory resisted the urge to lean up and touch her lips to his. "Do I get a tour of the building? I'm eager to put things in their place. My new friend, Alandriel, wants to help after her clinic shifts."

"That's a good idea. It will take a small army to clean the dust from these books."

They walked slowly to the back, passing rows of new bookshelves that smelled of fresh pine and varnish. His shoulder brushed against hers and at the last row, he turned abruptly, grabbed her arms, and claimed her mouth with his. One hand went to her back. The other cupped the back of her head. The kissing grew more intense. Rory's body tingled and burned, not from heat but from desire. Better judgment reared its head again, and she broke free. Rory straightened her sweater, and Jake looked slightly embarrassed.

"I'm sorry."

"It's okay."

"No, I'm going to try very hard not to do that again. It isn't fair."

She moved toward the front door, glancing at the clock above it. "Really, it's okay. Captain Barton will be back in a little while. I can get a head start. Clean the office ... and my desk."

"All right. I'll call you soon. I promise. Have fun with all of this. Let me know if you need anything. Anything at all. I'll arrange it."

"I will."

He left, and Rory felt both loss and relief. It got to her. The wanting. The physical need for intimacy, laughter, companionship. She knew Jake may not be available to fill that void. She was realizing the people of the Briar might not even allow it.

Her office was a small, closed-off room with a pass-through window to the long front counter where she would spend most of her time. It was obvious a cleaning crew had already removed the construction mess, and the place looked quite tidy. Crates of books lined the middle aisle. She would have to purchase office supplies and get someone with computer knowledge to train her so she could inventory each book.

The door swung open and Quinn strode in, carrying a huge, beautiful blue globe on a dark wood stand. Her heart jumped, and appreciation glowed in her eyes.

"Let me go wash the dust from my hands."

She returned and rushed over to gently trace the lines representing raised terrain, hills and mountains. She spun the glorious sphere around and couldn't stop smiling. "I want it to sit here, right where everyone will see it when they come in. Thank you so much."

"I have a small one to put in your office. I know how you love them. Do you have plans tonight? I mean, nothing big. Let me cook for you."

"You cook, captain?"

"Love to! It's a passion of mine, and I hardly ever get to share it. Please do me the honor."

She accepted the offer, as she was longing for more conversation.

CHAPTER FIVE

R ory came back to her apartment to find a folded note taped to her door. It simply stated

Look in the closet. —Jake.

Inside, there were dresses, tops, bottoms, and gowns in shades of gray, blue, and green. She bubbled inside, feeling the costly materials. She chose a simple gray sweater dress to wear to dinner. On the floor of the closet were dressy heeled shoes along with sleek boots and a type of shoe with laces she'd never seen before. She took out the tall, supple leather boots and slid them on. There were drawers in the closet she hadn't opened before that contained undergarments. They obviously weren't for everyday wear. Satin and lace and so small. She laughed, wondering who was supposed to see her in them. She pulled out a pair of thin, shiny stockings and decided to try them out, so she tugged off the boots, and fell in love with the smoothness of the stockings over her legs. She felt like a different person suddenly and was grateful. Rory figured she was only going next door and decided to walk over barefoot.

The smell of seasoned meat permeated the hallway. Music played on the other side of the door, and she could hear Quinn singing along. She smiled and listened for a minute. Rory wanted to see him instead of imagining him, so she tried the door, and it wasn't locked. She quietly slipped inside and saw his back facing her. He was singing out loud and moving his hips to the beat as he stirred a steaming pot. She let out an audible giggle, and he jumped and spun around.

"Rory! Shit! You scared me." He laughed. She laughed hard with him.

He looked down at her cute stockinged feet. "Well, aren't you a sight for sore eyes. Love the dress. Love the fact that you are here."

He glided over, kissed her forehead, and escorted her to the counter stool.

"Meatballs, noodles all slathered in tomato sauce so decadent you'll cry."

"Mmm. Can't wait. This looks really good, Quinn."

He poured two glasses of dark liquid, and they clinked them together before taking sips.

"Ah. This is wine from the grapes of the lost cities of the south. We lucked out on finding a winery that hadn't been ransacked after the first big battle. We're trying to cultivate the plants we brought from the land in our vine-yards, but only time will tell if we can pull it off."

"I know the wars were awful and many were lost, but the Briar seems to have the best of the best. I feel lucky to be accepted here. My new friend, Alandriel, told me about her mother and the children who are being born for repopulating. The doctor also told me I would never have children, but I already knew that was probably the case. I don't know why I'm telling you. I'm sorry."

"No. Don't be sorry. I don't mind. I want to get to know you. I want you to know me, and I never want people to know me." He looked down. "I ... I have, what you might say, a reputation. As a lush. I like drinking to excess. Partying, women. I mean, I am all in when I'm doing my job, but other times, I fear I overindulge. After I behaved badly toward you, and shit, I didn't even know you, something clicked inside. I ... want to be different. You make me want to be different."

There was sincerity in his eyes. She understood his wanting to be reinvented as someone, something different. She also felt his want to be more intimate with her.

"Quinn, I want us to trust each other. I don't have many to trust in this world. Can I trust you? Can we share things? Have fun? Grow a relationship that matters?"

A slow smile spread across his beautiful face. "I would like nothing more. I promise to earn your trust. I honor your feelings over my own. I'm also starving. Let's eat."

They laughed again and started to devour the food.

Quinn told her about all kinds of music and tuned the radio to a jazz station. Rory loved it. They went out to the balcony and leaned on the cool metal rail to see the cityscape at night. Their building backed up to the Lake of Peace. It was manmade, which meant the bright blue water was as still as glass unless there happened to be a storm brewing. A metal pier stretched halfway across the lake. Lights glittered on the surface.

Rory broke the easy silence. "So, tell me about the plays coming up."

"You know what? I don't even know what they're about, but I can find out. There's one in two weeks. Will you go with me?"

She turned around and propped her elbows on the rail. "Sure, and don't tell me. It will be a surprise. What do I wear?"

"Let me take care of that, if you will." His eyes looked both sleepy and sexy.

The music flowing through the open glass doors turned fast and fun, and Quinn took her in his arms and swung her around. She hung on and laughed and laughed and laughed. He was a great dancer. Their bodies moved together naturally. When it slowed, they kept going, clinging a little closer. Rory laid her head on his shoulder as he swayed. His soft cotton shirt smelled like fresh laundry soap. Quinn's mouth and nose nestled her hair, and he took in her scent of honeysuckle.

All of a sudden, Quinn's door crashed open with a loud bang, and Jacoby rushed in with a guard, looking around frantically. They jumped and released each other quickly.

"Rory! Oh, god, I couldn't find you. I tried calling you but got no answer, and when Quinn didn't answer either, I had to come myself to look for you. Why didn't you answer your communicator?" His angry face turned. "Quinn?"

Quinn attempted to apologize. "I'm sure Rory left hers next door. The music was loud and ... Sorry! Sorry, I just ..." he stammered.

Rory touched Quinn's arm but looked at Jacoby. "Major, can we speak in the hall?"

They stepped out. Quinn poured another glass of wine and downed it in one gulp.

"Jake, I am truly sorry. I didn't think I would be hearing from you tonight. Quinn offered to cook dinner, and—" She stopped and shook her head, looking for an explanation for what he had walked in on. "I will carry my communicator with me if I know you may need to speak with me."

Jacoby looked a bit pained. "I knew I would do this. I knew it would be like this. I don't have adequate time for you, and I am kidding myself to think you will wait for me."

He tilted her chin up. "Just ... just be careful. Guard your heart. Don't let Quinn drink too much. Don't forget me."

His last words cut her core. Forget him? Was that it? The end? "Forget you? I only just arrived. Jake, I have feelings for you I have never felt before. I trust you with my life. I hope we won't ever be truly apart from each other for long. I don't know what the future holds, but I know I could never forget you."

Jacoby knocked on the door twice, and the guard came out. "I'll talk to you soon. I'm glad you're okay."

And with that, he and the guard were gone.

Rory sighed and went back in to find Quinn slumped down on his couch, looking frazzled. He didn't move as she curled up on the green velvet next to him.

His eyes apologized. His eyebrows raised.

Rory laughed.

Quinn laughed. "Oh, shit. What just happened? I feel like we're in trouble now. Ha!"

"Maybe I need a little trouble in my life. I won't leave that damn communicator behind again," Rory joked. "I'm sorry your very nice dinner was interrupted. I hope the door isn't broken."

"Oh, it's fine. Well, we're keeping the major general on his toes." They giggled again.

Rory yawned. "Thank you for everything. We must do this again."

"With a different ending," Quinn pointed out, smirking.

"Yes, please. I can see myself out. Talk to you soon."

She stood, walked around the back of the couch, and leaned down to kiss the top of his head before exiting. Quinn was smitten.

Rory found her communicator on the kitchen counter, but nothing else disturbed. She had conflicting emotions spinning in her heart. Jake all but said he wasn't going to be around. Quinn was turning into quite the surprise. She had lots of work to do in the library. Her library. She went to bed happy to start over in the morning. It would be a new day with new adventures.

❧❧❧❧❧❧

The library sat directly across from the Central Military Office. Rory knew Jacoby had an office there and probably kept a close watch. Quinn had one as well. He often left the CMO right before she headed out.

The first half of her days flew by, and Alandriel showed up as promised after lunch. The books kept them occupied, and they resisted looking through each one even though they wanted to, fearing they'd never finish. The pair decided to stop at five in the evening and agreed to the same schedule each week, excluding Saturday. Alandriel had that day free, and Rory wanted to keep it that way.

On their time off, Alandriel took Rory around the city to help her get acclimated. She would be attending the theater, as well, with a date who worked directly under Quinn and asked Rory if they could make it a double date.

Rory made a habit during these two weeks of stopping for a warm roll and cider on her daily walk home. She continued through the city center onto the same pier that stretched across the lake and led straight to her building. It was all connected. She was glad it was easy to not get lost.

One Friday, Rory was happy to reach the end of her working day. She had stayed a couple of hours late, and it was now dark outside. The city would be lit up adequately for her to make it home just fine.

She backed out of the front door and was locking it when she felt light fingertips on her elbow. She screamed with a jump.

"Shhh, Rory. It's me," Quinn said with half a laugh.

"Damnit, Quinn! Don't do that again!" she scolded.

His hand went to his heart as he smirked, trying not to laugh. "Never. I'm sorry. You didn't leave when I was headed out, and I wanted to make sure you got back safely."

"You waited out here the whole time?"

"Well, I grabbed a bite at the market, but yes. Can I walk you home? You still going to the lake?"

She squinted. "How do you know I'm going to the lake?"

"We leave at the same time every day. I ... sort of ... follow you. I know it sounds bad, but I promise it's only because I feel protective of you. After I get up to my apartment, I can see you down on the pier. I don't

3001

watch you the whole time. Just long enough to see you're there."

For some reason, Rory didn't mind his protective prying. She hadn't spoken to Jake since he had busted through Quinn's door.

It was like Quinn could see her thoughts. "Have you heard from Jacoby?"

She looked down at the gray pavement under their feet. "No," she said quietly.

Quinn put an arm around her. "Rory, I have something for you." She looked up at his smiling eyes. He was very handsome and looked pleased with himself. He squeezed her shoulder. "Have you ever ridden a bicycle?"

Rory laughed. "No, but I have seen them around the city. They intrigued me."

"Maybe we can give it a go Sunday. That's when most of us ride in the park."

They reached the foyer, and he told her to expect a special delivery in the morning. She remembered he was taking care of her theater outfit.

She nodded in agreement, and Quinn went up to his place as she continued toward the water.

🙣🙣🙣🙣🙣

She slept. She slept very late. A heavy knock on the door woke her. It had to be almost noon. She stretched and rolled out of her beloved bed, putting on her black satin robe. A large white box sat beside her door. She took it to the bed and lifted the lid. On top lay a piece of black paper inscribed in silver:

> *Adorn yourself with this. Don't*
> *forget your heels this time.*

She giggled and folded back the white tissue paper to find a gorgeous red velvet dress. It was strapless and would stop just above her knees. The color was very much like the dress she had worn at the Crossroads

69

the night she danced with Jacoby. The memory was bittersweet for only a moment.

Her communicator signaled a call. "Good morning. Did you get my box?" Quinn's tone was raspy and heated.

"I did. It is too beautiful. I may just wear it all day." She laughed.

"Oh, well I will be thinking about you in it all day, then."

She fanned herself, clearing her throat. "What time will we be leaving? Alandriel is coming over to do something with this hair of mine. It is in desperate need of taming."

"Will you wear it down for me? I can still smell that honeysuckle."

Rory sank to the bed, crossing her legs, feeling warmth down below. "Um ... sure. Yes."

Quinn toned it down, thankfully. "I'll be over at six. See you then, darling."

Alandriel came over early to teach Rory how to use her appliances. Rory couldn't eat from the carts in the city center forever. They baked bread and made an easy noodle soup. Alandriel told her all about the other plays and concerts she had attended, then they took turns showering. The bathroom countertop couldn't be seen for all of Alandriel's date night necessities, as she put it. Rory had to admit, her favorites were the black eyelash serum and glossy red lip stain. She intended to apply an ample amount of her lotion, since Quinn so obviously loved it. Alandriel dressed in a long black satin gown, then ran a few drops of coconut oil through Rory's golden waves and let it dry naturally.

"That's the trick? A bit of coconut oil and I get these results? Wow."

Rory donned her stockings and laughed to herself as she slipped on the heels Quinn had requested.

Alandriel had been out with Quinn's first lieutenant, Dex, a handful of times. He was the highest-ranking member of the flight team who was a half. She admitted to Rory being surprised that she and the lieutenant had become so intimate.

"D and I have known each other our whole lives. We grew up on the farms. His mother was human too. She passed away a few years ago. He has always been my best friend, but we have seen each other a bit differently lately." Alandriel smiled. "We are both twenty-two now and thinking about the future, I guess. Since I have always had the vaccine, Dr. Lang thinks I should be able to have kids. The colony only allows halves to bear children with other halves."

Rory thought for a moment. "Makes sense from everything I've heard about growing a pure human population. They don't have to worry about me conceiving. I'm okay with that. I just wonder ... if I ever found someone again, would they want children?"

"Well, if that person turns out to be Captain Barton, I don't think you have to worry about that." Alandriel realized how she sounded. "I'm sorry. I shouldn't have said that. D said he has seen a change in Quinn lately. I'm sure it's all you. I'm so glad we are friends. My other friends are young and silly."

"Hey, I can be silly too." Rory laughed. "Thank you for your help today and all you do at the library. I think I should be available to help the nurses in a couple of weeks. I like to stay busy."

The girls heard a knock on the door, and Rory answered. There stood Dex in a gray suit with long coattails. He was gorgeous, with long, dark pewter-colored hair tied in the back. His eyes mirrored Rory's, and a wide smile spread across his face.

Quinn stepped out from his apartment in a black tuxedo, saluting the lieutenant. His gaze traveled from Rory's heels up to her crimson lips. His voice caught in his throat for a moment. "Uh, Lieutenant Dex Baxter, this is Ms. Rory Larken."

Dex took her hand. "The pleasure is all mine." He looked past Rory. "Alandriel! Wow! You are a vision." He went to her and they shared a short kiss.

Quinn grabbed Rory's hand and pulled her into the hallway. "Give us just a moment," he told the couple, shutting the door between them.

One hand caressed her arm. The other fingers twirled in her long waves. He was looking at her like he wanted to swallow her whole. "Wow. I mean, Rory." He sighed. "Shit. Sorry, you just look ... perfect. Wow."

Rory blushed, put her hand on his clean-shaven jaw-line, and pulled his head to hers so she could kiss his cheek. She lingered there, feeling her body buzzing a bit as he took in the scent he was obsessed with.

"Okay. All right. We should be going," he whispered. He straightened his lapels and patted the inside pocket of his coat. "I have my communicator." He laughed. "But the major general will probably be there too."

Rory hadn't thought about that. She brushed it away and decided to enjoy the evening. She was building a new life in a big, bright new colony, and she decided to live it to the fullest.

CHAPTER SIX

The four walked to a rail station just outside the building and took a train a few blocks to the theater. It was Rory's first train ride, and she loved the zoom. Plush upholstered booths and low lighting set a calming mood. Those who traveled farther were offered pastries and tea or ale. The others watched Rory's eyes scan her surroundings, and soon they arrived.

Quinn placed a hand on the small of her back as they walked up a huge granite staircase to towering, gilded Art Deco doors. They made a stop at the black-and-gold, shiny bar for bubbly champagne that tickled Rory's nose and tasted of berries. The crowd was getting thick, so Dex led them into the theater and to the front row to sit. The stage was about four feet above their seats and so close. Elegant crystal chandeliers glowed overhead. Deep navy blue covered every soft surface, from the carpet to the chairs to the stage curtains. The dark purple walls reminded her of the night sky. It was so moody and perfect.

Rory felt Quinn studying her and turned to him, smiling. He scanned her body over once more and reached for her hand, pulling it to his chest. Surprised, she felt familiar vibrations. He must have, too, because he suddenly had a puzzled but excited look in his eyes. Rory couldn't believe it. She had only felt that with Jake.

Quinn still stared, intertwining their fingers.

She blushed. "It's just a thing that happens sometimes. You know, a half thing, I guess." She wasn't sure how to explain. "Please don't be put off by it."

He shook his head and whispered, "Put off? Rory, I find it rather ... pleasurable." His eyes held hers, entranced. Soft orchestral music began, breaking the bond.

He sighed, directing his attention to the stage as the curtains parted. "All right then, here we go."

Rory liked making Quinn uncomfortable. She knew he wasn't quite sure what to do with her, and that gave her some control. She also wondered how it must be for Alandriel and Dex. Two halves. She laughed to herself, picturing them setting the colony on fire with their intimacy. The music swelled, and obnoxiously beautiful costumed actors glided together, singing in a language unknown to her. It didn't matter. The magic of it brought tears to her eyes, and she didn't realize she was squeezing Quinn's hand so hard. After four songs the curtains closed, signaling an intermission.

She let go and flexed her sore fingers as the lights came back up.

Quinn stood. "Fifteen minutes to stretch, drink, or, you know."

Rory nodded. "Yes, Alandriel and I will be back."

The two were making their way back when Rory felt a hand close around her wrist.

Alandriel turned, recognized the man first, and bowed her head a bit. "Major general."

He hadn't let go, and Rory turned to her. "Um, Alandriel, I will see you inside." She wasn't sure what to say. They just looked at each other for a few moments. Everyone else had noticed the pair. Rory glanced around for Quinn. Finally, Jacoby tugged her into a side room with a plaque on the door reading "Reel Room." They were alone in low light with shelves full of movie reels.

Jacoby let go and straightened. "Hello, Rory." He searched her eyes. He looked older and stressed. She knew what he needed when he took her hands in his.

"Close your eyes, Jake. Take a few deep breaths. Take my energy." She spoke in a soft, soothing voice. He did as she instructed, and his posture loosened. His shoulders relaxed and then he embraced her against his tall body. She let him.

Rory thought about Quinn, who was waiting and probably wondering where she was.

She pushed Jacoby back a little. "Okay. That's all I've got for now. I have to get back."

"Yes, I saw you with the captain." He let go and leaned down to kiss her.

"Wait." Her fingers stopped his lips. "I can't. Not tonight. I'm sorry. Call me. We should speak soon."

And with that, she left him alone.

The lights dimmed as she shuffled quickly down the aisle. Dex, Alandriel, and Quinn were chatting, but Rory got a look from Alandriel as she sat down. Quinn gave half a smile, and a cello cried to start the last act. Rory glanced over; his face was not as easy, so she claimed his hand this time and placed it in her lap. He settled down in his seat.

The final melancholy song had tears rolling down Rory's cheeks, and Quinn offered a handkerchief from his pocket. She dabbed her face, and he pushed a long, stray tendril of hair from her forehead and tucked it behind her ear.

"Did you like it?"

"It was glorious." She beamed up at him.

"Will you come back with me?"

"We'll see," she teased.

"Oh, we'll see? We shall see, all right," he replied with a determined look in his eyes.

Alandriel reached for her. "Wasn't it amazing? Wait until you see a comedy. You'll simply adore it."

Dex quietly spoke to Quinn, and he nodded in agreement. "The lieutenant and his fair lady will not be joining us for the ride home."

Alandriel hugged Rory. "I'll get my things tomorrow, if that's okay?"

"Of course. Thank you for everything, my friend."

After they split off, Quinn directed her back to the bar for another glass of champagne. About a third of the crowd did the same. The rest filtered out. She didn't see Jacoby again and was glad.

Quinn sat their empty flutes down. "No more. I'm trying to be upstanding, remember? You ready to go home?"

Home. Rory admitted to herself she already felt at home at the Briar. Such a city, she thought. The possibilities seemed endless here. Almost everything was falling into place. Everything except for the perilous balancing act between two men. One wild, free spirit. The other the most powerful human in the colony. The man who had to keep up appearances and transform into what the colony wished. Rory couldn't have it both ways.

They held on to a brass pole near the window of the train instead of sitting at one of the booths. Quinn watched her face. She wasn't looking at him. He didn't deserve her and never imagined he would have her, but her hand was in his. He glanced down at their intertwined fingers. When he raised his head, she was watching him. He smiled, and Rory felt his love.

She turned toward the door to watch the only other passenger leave the car. Quinn swayed behind her as the train moved again. So close she felt his heat. Heavy breath exited his lips, and it was warm against her neck. Rory leaned only an inch, and her back was against his chest. He let out a deeper breath, brushing his mouth behind her right earlobe. He splayed long fingers across her collarbone. The other hand covered the red velvet over her tummy, pressing the length of his body to hers.

He bowed his head to whisper in her ear. "Darling. Stay with me tonight."

Lips touched skin, and Rory melted. She slid around, her mouth ready to answer. The touching was intense, and they both knew she would honor his request.

They were still all over each other when they tumbled through Quinn's door. Rory had been sexually frustrated for months. No. Years. She took the lead, deftly releasing the buttons of his shirt and pinning him against the inside of the door. Her eyes glowed like stars in the dark room.

Quinn had been with plenty of women but never a half. That fact was not what made this encounter so new for him. Rory had become a friend. This was on a much higher level. To be with a lover he cared so deeply for was astounding. All other women were rubbish in comparison.

Rory felt wild with Quinn. She slowed the pace after his shirt was gone, kissing his neck and chest. He unzipped the back of her dress, and it fell to the floor. She looked exquisite in black lace. Rory adored the way he surveyed her with a smile on his lips. They paused, looking into each other's eyes.

His voice heated, he said, "Rory. I've never wanted anyone the way I want you. No one else has ever meant more."

She knew he was telling the truth. She put her hands around his face and kissed him sweetly, then whispered, "Take me to your bed."

He gently scooped her up and laid her down on the cool, beige cotton. City lights glinted through the window. He propped over her, continuing tender kisses. She raised up, scooted to the edge of the bed, and tugged his waistband open. He was tall and lean and beautiful. He ran his hands through her hair. He was erect and ready for her, as she knew he would be. She didn't want it to happen too fast, so she decided to show him he was her central focus. Rory took him into her hand and ran the other over his backside. As her mouth moved toward his member, he stopped her.

"Rory. Wait. You don't have to ..." He was used to women pleasuring him, then leaving. It was never intimate.

Rory smiled as though she read his mind. "I want to. I'm not going anywhere."

He relaxed a bit, and she continued to her destination. Her talented tongue very nearly sent him into oblivion. He couldn't bear it, halting her and panting. Now she smiled shyly, wiping her lips. Her naughty look made him laugh. She stood and turned around. Quinn kissed her shoulders as she slid off her underwear. Her nakedness bewitched him. He explored her neck, back, waist, hips. He licked behind her ear as he held her warm, soft breasts in his palms. Her body vibrated again, and he flung her around, picked her up again, and tossed her on the bed, laughing. She laughed, too, and welcomed him into her with no need to worry about heat or fire, only reckless abandon.

Rory rejoiced inside, feeling completely free for the first time in so long. She kept her leg over Quinn's hip, watched his satisfied face, and played with his short curls. His fingers made a circle around her knee cap. She knew he felt the energy she still emitted, but his face changed.

"You saw Jacoby, didn't you? That's why Alandriel returned alone." He stared at the ceiling.

She sighed. "I did. I didn't go looking for him. He found me."

"Do you mind that I asked?"

"No. I knew you would wonder where I was. Jake looks tired. I'm not even sure if he really cared about seeing me or if he just wanted my energy." She shifted to her side and touched his chin, drawing his attention to her eyes.

"You feel it too. When we traveled here, he would draw from it. It calmed him, and I was amazed because it had never happened before. I didn't mind sharing it, because it doesn't take much from me and it helped him. I want you to know we were never like this. This intimate. We did kiss. We shared a bed, because I was afraid of what might happen if I overheated alone. If I had lost control, started a fire on the airship, we would have all been in big trouble. I hadn't had a close friend in years. It was nice, but I'm not his and he never gave the notion that I was. We both knew things would be different here at the Briar."

Quinn looked calm now. "I understand. You saved his life, don't forget. I'm grateful he brought you here. I know you are close, and I won't stand in the way of that."

She put her fingers to his lips. "Quinn ... right here is where I want to be."

With a sly smile, Quinn reached out, dragging her on top, ready to go again. "I'm hungry, darling, and you taste so good."

❊❊❊❊❊

Rory woke to the sweet smell of waffles and peeked out of the bedroom, seeing Quinn, in only shorts and an apron, stirring batter in a big yellow bowl with his long, sexy fingers. He looked up, sensing her, and winked.

"There's a robe for you on the chair by the bed."

She padded into the bathroom to freshen up before returning to a finished golden stack ready to be consumed. Quinn sat on a stool and pulled her onto his lap, so she fed him the first bite.

"It will be hard living next door. I'll be knocking on your door, begging for breakfast."

"Mmm, only breakfast." He laughed and kissed her neck.

"Well ... Seriously, though. These are perfect."

"You are perfect. Still want to go to the park?"

"Um, yes, but I can't promise that I'll be any good at riding a bike."

"There's plenty to do there. Dex and Alandriel usually picnic, weather permitting. The stables are there. We could ride horses. You can ride a horse, right?"

"Of course! I'm an expert equestrian."

"Oh, really?"

"Mmm hmm," she hummed, getting up to rinse the dishes.

"I'll take care of that. Why don't you tiptoe over to your place and get into some clothes? Oh, and wear tennis shoes."

She looked puzzled.

"They have laces, thick soles made for sport, walking, running ... You know what? I'll be over in twenty minutes to help."

In her own room, Rory jumped in the shower, then ran coconut oil through her hair before tying it back. She picked out a cotton bra and panties but sat on the edge of the bed with a T-shirt in hand, contemplating what would be appropriate.

Quinn entered her room in long black shorts and a white tee. "Hi."

She raised her hand, questioning her decisions so far.

He pointed at it. "Yes, and ..." He went into her closet and pulled out blue shorts, socks, and the laced tennis shoes.

She dressed, and Quinn hugged her from behind, smelling her ponytail as they left her apartment.

The sun was shining bright, and the park teemed with halves and humans. More halves than Rory had ever seen all in one place, still outnumbered by humans, of course. Every couple was human with human, half with half. She and Quinn were the only mismatched pair, but she knew Quinn didn't care what others would think. They waved at Dex and Alandriel, who were stretched out on a blanket reading. Rory could see the gorgeous white stables. She had always loved the smell of a barn. The hay. The horses.

She nudged Quinn's arm in that direction. "Can we?"

"Of course."

She immediately recognized a large black stallion in the first stall, and he seemed to recognize her as he stuck his head over the half door for a nose rub.

"Oh, hi friend. Hello, beautiful Toby."

"Oh, yeah. You know this big boy." Quinn scratched behind the horse's ear.

A stable hand spoke up. "Ma'am, do you know this horse? He really needs a run, but he won't let just anyone ride him."

"Oh, um, I'm not sure the major general would want me to."

"Oh, ma'am, he won't mind. I'm sure he will appreciate it. I'll saddle him up."

The man led Toby to the outdoor arena, where Quinn mounted a white mare next to an open gate. Rory easily hoisted herself up. When the horse didn't make a fuss, the stable hand gave her a thumbs up.

Quinn got an adventurous look in his eyes. "Wanna get out of here?"

Rory nodded, and they took off through a field of wildflowers.

When they returned, they joined Dex and Alandriel for a picnic while a band played live music on a pavilion before going home.

"Want to sleep over tonight?" Quinn asked casually as they rode the elevator back up to their floor.

Rory stopped when they stepped out and leaned against the wall. "Maybe it would be wise to take things a bit slower. Not that I don't really, really want to ..." She reached out and tugged his shirt, bringing him closer.

Quinn placed a hand on the wall behind her head and the other on her waist. He licked his lips. "Can I walk you home after work tomorrow?"

Her answer was obvious when she closed the small space between them and planted her lips on his. Her tongue ran over his bottom lip, then moved on to explore his mouth. Quinn seized her up, and she wrapped her legs around his hips. He practically growled and carried her down the hall into her apartment. His body fell on top of hers on the couch. Both enjoyed the touching, the tasting. Rory's body pulsated, while his throbbed. It would be so easy to give in to lust, but Quinn slowed the pace.

He had a spark in his eye when he looked down at her. "Trust."

She held on to his sides, keeping him in place. "Trust ... yes, and friendship."

He pulled her up to straddle his lap. "Mmm, your body and my body."

He nuzzled her neck as he did often, and she squeezed him tight. Holding on to each other felt right.

Quinn mumbled into her ear, "I should probably be saying good night now." He stood and reluctantly sat her on her feet. "Good night, darling Rory. Sleep well."

CHAPTER SEVEN

R ory's communicator beeped before she had set her alarm to go off.

"Hello? Rory?" It was Jake.

"Oh, hello. Good morning. Is everything all right?"

"Yes. I ... wanted to come and see the library today, if that's okay."

"Yes. I mean, you are the major general. You don't really need my permission, do you?"

He chuckled. "Well, no. I guess I don't. I'll see you later, then."

Rory and Alandriel had stocked enough books on the shelves that they had begun to let people check them out. Everyone had been knocking on the door asking for them. Quinn arranged for a familiar face to assist Rory with the computer system. Jimena, the girl who had checked Rory into the colony, was a great teacher, and Rory caught on easily. Jimena had a deep love for books and asked to stay on full time.

It was after lunch when Jacoby walked in. Rory could see him from her office. He stopped, gave the globe a whirl with his finger, and smiled. His eyes took in the space, looking pleased. Several individuals sat at reading desks, while a couple of groups of students from the school browsed the aisles. Rory came around the counter, tucking her hair behind her ear.

"Hello, major," she said politely.

"Ms. Larken." He searched her face, then glanced around to see everyone staring at them.

Rory whispered, "Would you like to speak in my office?"

He followed her, and she pulled down the pass-through door. Rory sat on the edge of her desk. Jacoby removed his cape. He had on civilian clothes. He looked thinner than the last time she had seen him, but still so handsome.

"So, how are you? The place looks amazing. I knew you would bring it to life. Have plenty of help?" He rambled on, obviously nervous. "I know Jimena. She is so smart with technology. Oh, and thank you for taking Toby out. I haven't had much time. I'm grateful ..." He finally took a breath and came to stand directly in front of her. "How are you?"

Rory straightened. "The library has brought me so much joy. I have made the best friends, and everything is falling into place. I don't know why I was so nervous before. And the vaccine! I don't even have to worry about being a hazard."

He looked serious. "But I still felt you. The other night. I was hoping I could still feel you."

There was a buzz between them, and Rory took his hand. "Is this what you came for? Is this what you need?"

His eyes closed, then opened when he realized what she meant. "Rory, I'm not just using you. I promise. I never wanted us apart. Things are complicated. Always so complicated."

"Jake, I'm seeing Quinn. You probably already know that, but I ... feel torn. I feel a loyalty to you, and you ... you mean a lot to me, and you know I cherish our friendship and our connection. It's so easy with Quinn. He's always around, and he is actually a very caring, beautiful soul. I know he would give his life for me. I haven't heard from you in so long."

He took her other hand but looked pained and spoke somberly. "I didn't bring you here as my prize. I know I am a selfish man. I admit I want you. I wish there was another way. A way where I didn't have to see you with someone else. I also know I could never ask you to wait for me. You shouldn't have to. I can tell you are happy. I'm shocked as hell it's Quinn making you happy."

"Jake. I'm going to say this one time and then I'll not say it again ... I do love you. I think I'll always love you. You are important to me, and I want you to be okay. It matters to me to know you are all right."

He smiled and embraced her. "Oh, look at us. We are like a fish and a bird, never to be."

She gave him extra energy as best as she could, holding on to him.

"If you ever need this, come to me."

He took it, and Rory wondered how long it might be until the next time. He heard her sniffling and pulled back to see her face. "Don't. I'm not worth your tears. I'll start, too."

She laughed a little, knowing this was a chapter about to close, as she wiped her face.

"I'm serious. If you ever need me. I know you have a big job to do here for the colony, and if I can help in this strange way, I'm here."

"I know. I'll be around. I promise not to pry too much either, but I'll be around." He took hold of her one more time. "I love you."

With that, he let go and was gone.

He really had a way of leaving her emotions in tangles. She sighed and smoothed her sweater as Jimena stuck her head in the door. Rory lifted the pass-through again.

"Everything all right?" Jimena asked, smiling like she had seen a king.

"Yes. He was just making sure everything is tidy and to our liking. He complimented your intelligence," she said with a wink.

"I know. He thanked me as he was walking out. Gosh, he's so lovely," she swooned.

Rory laughed. "Lovely. Alandriel used the word grumpy, I think."

They laughed together as Alandriel came in the front door. "I saw major moody leaving just now," she joked.

Jimena and Rory busted out laughing harder, while Alandriel just looked curious about what in the world was so funny.

�֍✖֍✖֍✖

Quinn and Rory leaned on the rail of the pier, looking at the lake. They stood arm to arm, hip to hip. He rested his forehead on hers. She closed her eyes and took a deep breath.

He spoke softly. "I know I'm not your first choice. I know there is something between you and Jake that I could never have with you, but I'm falling in love with you, darling. Could you ever love me?"

He was so sincere. Rory couldn't deny she felt at peace with where they were. She had grown to care for him a great deal. He had made a complete turnaround since they first met. She reached over and took his hand, lacing their fingers together.

He whispered, "Oh, Rory," and pulled her against his chest, crushing his mouth to hers. It was a hot, intense kiss filled with all of the passion she had to offer.

She held his face in her hands, wanting him to know she meant what she was saying, and she couldn't believe she was saying it twice in one day.

"Quinn ... I love you too. Please don't ever think that I don't. We are alike in many ways. Our hearts aren't much different. I understand your heart. I know you love me. It's easy to feel. I want to be with you."

"Let's go home." He held on tighter, cherishing her words.

✖֍✖֍✖֍

Rory practically lived at Quinn's place. He always left before her in the mornings, but they walked home

86

together every night, cooked dinner, danced, laughed, made love.

One afternoon, Quinn slipped into her office, closing the door and the window. He hurried over to where she was sitting in her desk chair and kissed her neck, laughing. They enjoyed playing with each other. He made it so easy to love him.

She giggled, pushing him away. "What are you doing here? This is quite a nice surprise."

He sat on the edge of the desk near her. "We have news." His face went serious.

"A small assembly of dragons was found beyond our borders. We have had soldiers watching them closely. Their numbers are double what we anticipated, and they are heavily armed. It looks like we are going to be back under a code red here in the Briar ... and I'll be leading the airstrike when the time is right. Jacoby will be going as well. I'll be late at a meeting tonight."

Rory stood up between his knees, embracing him hard. She began to sob.

"Darling, it's all right. It's all right."

"How long? How long till you leave? How long will you be gone?"

"There's a bit of strategic planning to do, and my men are readying the fleet. We have a couple of weeks."

She squeezed harder. "Quinn."

He pulled her back and gripped her shoulders. "It's okay. I can't have you worrying like this. You get yourself a hot cider and some of that bread you love. Get me some, too, and I'll see you at home."

He kissed her hard and went back to the CMO.

Of course she worried. News spread fast, and people were whispering about war around the library. Rory, Jimena, and Alandriel decided to limit the hours the library would be open so they could go help at the infirmary if needed. The Briar was on edge. Everyone could feel it.

Around midnight, Quinn found Rory out on the balcony in her blue satin nightgown, breathing in the night air. He wrapped himself around her from behind.

She moaned, "I missed you. I couldn't sleep."

He tugged her back inside and pulled her down on top of himself on the couch. She laid her head on his chest, listening to his heartbeat, and spoke first.

"Poor Alandriel. I think she almost wore a hole in the carpet at the library, pacing back and forth. Dex wants to marry her before he leaves, but she won't do it. I tried to talk her into it."

"That's an idea."

"What?"

Quinn played with her left ring finger.

"You and I. We could ..."

"Get married? Hmm ..." She had to admit her stomach did a flip in a good way. *Why not*, she thought.

He knew she was seriously considering the notion, and wanted to seal the deal. "I'd marry you right now if you said yes."

Rory sat up, straddling him, looking at his face. She couldn't help but smile, and he glowed up at her. She traced his bottom lip with her thumb.

"If you ask me properly, I just might."

Quinn leapt up, settling her straight on the couch, and kneeled in front of her. He reached out for her hand and placed it on his heart.

"Rory Larken, would you do me the incredible honor of becoming my wife?"

Her hand sent soothing pulses through his chest.

"Yes, Quinn. I love you."

He scooped her up off of her feet and swung her around, laughing. "You just made me the happiest being in the universe. I love you, darling."

"Can we do it before you leave? I don't want to wait."

"Of course. We can do it as soon as we want. Shit! I can't believe this. I never thought I would feel like this."

Rory loved his enthusiasm and sincere love for her. "We can talk about it while you cook me one of those mouthwatering omelets in the morning."

Neither Quinn nor Rory cared about a big fuss, so they decided to meet Dex and Alandriel at sunset to exchange vows. Since the wars, the colony had recognized a marriage as long as there were at least two witnesses and a signed certificate of marriage.

Alandriel and Jimena took Rory to the mercantile to buy a new dress. She chose a long, floral, burned velvet gown in deep crimson, Quinn's favorite color. She left her hair down in loose curls. Jimena followed her friends, and Quinn and Dex looked dashing in gray suits at the end of the pier as Rory and Alandriel strolled arm in arm to meet them. Rory carried a bouquet of red roses and tucked one in the pocket of Quinn's coat when she took her place beside him.

He couldn't help himself and grabbed her for a quick kiss, whispering, "Darling, you look ravishing."

Alandriel took the bouquet, and Dex began the informal ceremony. "We come together this evening to join in holy matrimony—I never thought I'd say this—Captain Quinn Barton and Ms. Rory Larken. Do you have any words for one another?"

Quinn turned to her, took both of her hands, and grinned. "Rory. My Rory. What can I say? You have tamed a beast. I don't deserve you. I vow to you to move only forward from this day, forgetting the past and embracing the bright future with you, the only woman I've ever truly loved. I will adore you, protect you, and never take you for granted."

Rory's eyes glistened. "Quinn, my love I pledge to you for the rest of our days. You are mine and I am yours. I treasure you, and you can always be assured my love for you is unwavering. I choose you."

Dex removed a ring from his pocket and placed it in Quinn's palm. Rory gasped when Quinn slid the shiny gold band on her finger. A huge ruby glittered up at her. Jimena reached over and gave Rory Quinn's simple gold band. She did love him so, and he felt it when she put on his ring and held on to his hand. She overflowed with positive energy, and he wished to run away with her at that moment and make love.

"Do you, Rory, take Quinn as your forever life partner?"

"I do."

"And do you, Quinn, take Rory as your forever life partner?"

"I absolutely do."

"By the authority vested in me, I now pronounce you husband and wife. You may—"

Quinn didn't wait. He threw Rory into a dip and kissed her deeply.

"—kiss the bride."

Dex and Alandriel laughed and shared a kiss. He leaned to her ear. "When I get back, be ready. We are getting married if I have to drag you to the altar."

Alandriel nodded. "All right, all right."

When Quinn let Rory go, the group of friends hugged and congratulations were given. They made their way back to the building, where a long black car was waiting for them.

"What's this?" Rory inquired.

"This is the ride to our honeymoon. We will be staying at the Crown Hotel tonight. I packed you a bag and everything. Just you and I, as husband and wife."

The Crown towered twenty stories into the sky. A gentleman took their luggage, following them into the expansive black-and-gold lobby. Quinn checked them in and led her to the elevator and the room. It was a large suite with a living room, bathroom, kitchen, and bedroom. Rory could see a bubbling, steamy bath out on the balcony. Vases of white gardenias sat on every surface, filling the room with a seductive scent. Shades of deep magenta and teal created a perfect mood for romance. Quinn took the bags to the bedroom and returned, lighting candles on the coffee table. He tuned a radio to a station with slow, sexy music, and a woman pushed a brass cart covered with bread, wine, and chocolate candies through the door. Rory took off her heels and plucked a truffle from the silver tray. Quinn took bite from her fingers, and she had the rest as he poured the wine.

"Thank you for this. My husband." She slid her arms around his neck, and he swayed to the song. "Sounds good, doesn't it?"

"Mmm, yes. My beautiful wife. This. This will carry me on wings while I'm gone."

"Uh-uh. We're not talking about that tonight. You will be back soon, and we will live happily ever after."

"Oh yes. Definitely. Let's talk about this dress." He ran his hands over her back, pulling her as close as possible.

"Kiss me, you beast," she joked.

He did so with fervor.

After an hour of what Quinn called "the most life-altering experience I've ever had," the bride and groom finished off the food and wine before sleeping wrapped up in each other.

CHAPTER EIGHT

Quinn stepped on to the elevator at the CMO to ride up to the third floor, where a battle planning meeting would be held. It made a stop on the second floor, and Jacoby joined him. Quinn nervously ran a hand through his hair. Jacoby's breath caught in his chest and his heart fell when he saw the gold band. The doors opened, and Jacoby pulled Quinn to the side.

He cleared his throat. "So, have some good news, captain?"

Quinn looked down. "I do. It happened yesterday, actually."

Jacoby held out a hand. "Congratulations."

Quinn obliged. "Thank you, sir."

Jacoby paused, unsure of what to say. He felt anger, regret, and bitterness that he wasn't standing in Quinn's shoes right now.

"Shall we?" Quinn motioned for them to follow the rest of the men into the boardroom.

❖❖❖❖❖❖

Quinn walked across the street to the library as soon as the meeting ended. He nodded to Jimena, who sat at the front counter, and spotted Rory speaking with a small group of children on a blue, circular rug.

"Oh, Captain Barton, congratulations! Rory has been beaming all day." Jimena smiled.

"As have I." He winked, and Jimena swooned over the romance of it all.

Rory returned to the front, and he followed her into the office, shutting the door. "Hello, love. I missed you," he said into her neck while sprinkling kisses over her collarbone.

"Mmm, yes. I missed you too. How was the meeting?"

"Fine. A boring old meeting. I saw Jake. He figured it out, of course. Shook my hand and offered his congratulations, although he's not happy about it. I don't blame him."

"Well that was fast, but good he knows. He won't treat you differently, will he?"

"No, love. Don't worry about that. We have always worked well together. I'll just be in a much better mood than him now," he joked. "I have to get back. My flight team has a short conference, but I'll be here to walk you home."

"Great. Love you."

❊❊❊❊❊❊❊

The days flew by. Rory had never been so happy, but she felt the stress of Quinn's impending departure a little more with each passing day. Each hug lasted a little longer. Each kiss brought forth more and more energy from her body, and the passion they shared when they were intimate couldn't be described.

A plan was in place. The flight team was scheduled to lead an airstrike on Friday in hopes of dramatically slashing the number of dragons before ground troops advanced. That meant only five days remained until Quinn departed. Jacoby would safely follow along the battle lines to monitor the progress in a huge rover tank the size of a small house.

Rory frequented the infirmary at the intake headquarters to get familiar with the nurses and doctors and learned about a few new medical discoveries that made dressing wounds quick and easy while Quinn attended strategy meetings. Rory spoke to Alandriel at the infirmary, but every free second Alandriel could find, she spent with Dex. Jimena kept the library open for a couple of hours in the mornings. The dwellers of the Briar were on high alert and stayed home more than usual. School officials decided to close for a break while the majority of the troops were away.

On Quinn's last night home, Rory turned on classical music, lit candles with her fingertips, and ordered delivery from International Café, which she spread out on the counter. She planned on pampering and pleasuring Quinn as soon as he walked through the door. She slithered into a one-piece undergarment in red lace and tied a white silk robe around her waist. Rory couldn't stop glancing at his flight team bags that sat packed on the bedroom floor. He was all set to leave the next day.

Quinn walked in and looked thrilled as she took the books and computer from his hands. She sat them down, then slid herself against his body, kissing his neck.

"Darling. Oh my god, you are astounding. Look at all of this. Look at you." He kissed her and she loosened his necktie. His hands grabbed her buttocks, gliding over the silk, and he squeezed, pressing her against his erection.

"Oh, Quinn. I'm dying to have you. We can eat after."

She unbuttoned his pants as they desperately touched every inch of one another. He was soon naked, but paused after tossing her robe to the floor. The red lace entranced him. Long fingers rubbed over the center of her sweet spot, and she writhed with pleasure. Quinn pressed her back to the wall and made that sultry circular motion, driving her very near the edge. His hot mouth passed over the material covering her breasts, and she shuddered. He slid his fingers underneath the lace and rubbed harder. He found her wet and wanting, moaning his name. Quinn pushed the fabric to the side and penetrated her slick lips. He smoothly moved in and out at a tantalizing pace. He was all hers, she all his. Rory tightened inside, and his motion escalated. The vibrating pulses drove him to orgasm. Her hands were in his hair, and she threw her legs around his waist, clamping as she came.

He kept hold of her and moved to the couch, where he sat with Rory still wrapped around him. She squeezed him again with every muscle she had, treasuring the feeling. Quinn held his lover sweetly, caressing her with such care and compassion. She pulled back a little to appreciate his beautiful face and kissed him tenderly.

"I love you, Quinn Barton. I'll think of you every minute of every day that passes."

He kissed her back fervently. "Your love is the reason I wake in the morning, my darling. I do everything for you."

Rory smoothed his curls and couldn't get enough physical touch. He closed his eyes, and she sent her vibrations coursing through his skin. He shivered a little. "Rory. I'll miss your tingle."

They laughed. Her palms lay flat on each side of his face, then traveled to his neck and continued downward to rest on his chest. She tried to memorize the rhythm of his heart. A tear fell and landed on his belly.

"Oh, darling. Thank you for loving me more than I ever thought I would be."

Rory shook her head. "You mean the world to me. I'm the lucky one."

❖❖❖❖❖❖

Jacoby turned up his glass, emptying it in one gulp. His mood was melancholy, his thoughts dark. He should be composing a good pep talk to deliver to the troops in the morning, but no matter who he spent time with, what function he attended, how much liquor he drank, his soul remained consumed by thoughts of her. Too many of his evenings were ruled by depression and sleeplessness. He knew it was becoming a problem. The mirror reflected his troubles. He almost broke the damn thing on a particularly low night. She could have been his. His heart would always be hers. He longed to see her, touch her, hold her, feel her. He wished he could go to her, claim her as his own. If only he could turn back time.

✵✵✵✵✵

Rory and Quinn walked hand in hand into the military base camp in silence. Neither of them wanted to say goodbye. He kept her hand in his even when he greeted members of his flight team. He couldn't let go yet.

Rory noticed Alandriel and broke the bond. Quinn winked and kissed her forehead before they separated.

"Hi, D. Hi, Alandriel," Rory said.

They both appeared nervous. Alandriel grabbed on for a hug, and Rory consoled her, keeping an arm around her shoulders. "They'll be okay. They will be back before we know it."

Alandriel was holding back tears. Dex went to join uniformed men and women who stood around in a group chatting while their wives, husbands, and partners watched stoically.

Jacoby strode in, and he and Quinn disappeared behind a door marked "War Room." The air was thick with anticipation. The whirring sound of battleships starting up thudded outside. Dex returned to Alandriel and pulled her aside to say goodbye.

Quinn stuck his head out from behind the war room door and motioned for Rory to come. He stepped out, looking serious.

"Jacoby asked to speak privately with you. Do you mind? I'll be right here."

She slowly nodded and took a deep breath before going in.

Jacoby remained on the opposite side of a U-shaped conference table but smiled when he saw her face. Rory noticed dark circles under his eyes, and his body was even leaner now.

"Thank you for agreeing to meet with me. I'm being selfish again."

She gave a half smile and crooked a finger for him to come. He took his time getting to her, burning the sight of her into his brain to remember later. He stopped in front of her, and she took his hands as she had many times before. He closed his eyes. Her heart broke a little. She studied him while he took her energy. For a few moments, her mind played out what might have been. He took in a few deep breaths, and she tugged his arms around her waist, bringing him intimately close. Her head rested on his hard chest, and his pulse escalated. Jacoby propped his chin on top of her head; that familiar honeysuckle reminded his senses of the past. Rory smoothed the back of his uniform shirt, signaling their time was almost up.

"Jake, I'll be thinking of you. I'm glad you wanted to see me. I want you to take care of yourself. You have to be strong for the Briar. The colony needs you. I need you ..."

"Shhh..." He rubbed a hand through her silky hair and gave her a solid embrace. "We have to get you back to Quinn." He turned her loose and smiled. "I love you, Rory."

"I love you too, Jake."

She went straight to Quinn, and Jacoby nodded to him before heading out to the rover tank. The flight team boarded their battleships and ascended to the clouds, one after the other.

The pair stood by the big, open bay door. Quinn crushed her mouth with his. He had to leave, and her body felt it.

"I love you. I'll be waiting for you."

"My heart stays here." And with that, he lifted his chin and strolled to his own battleship. Rory watched as a part of her soared out of sight.

Alandriel found her, and they clung to each other, faces wet with tears. One of the husbands who had been left behind passed out tissues to the emotional group as each of them slowly exited the building to return home alone.

"Rory, I don't want to go home. It's early. We won't be needed at the infirmary for at least two days or more, hopefully. Let's go see the babies."

"Babies?"

"Yes! We can hop on the train and get our minds off everything."

"Okay. I have never held a baby before."

�֍✧✧✧✧✧

They came to a stop in front of a tall fence. The sign over the heavily guarded gate read "Brick Yard."

"It's called the brick yard so that if any dragons get a map of the Briar, they won't know the location of the children. The council is smart."

They flashed medical badges and gained entry. It looked like a quaint little town inside the enclosure, with small, separate homes, fenced yards, a small mercantile, a mother–baby clinic, and a school. Rory remembered there would only be human children here and caught sight of three young boys with bright red hair walking into the school with a woman. Rory had only seen one man with the same hair color, and he was high ranking.

"Colonel Lewis. I know you see the resemblance."

Rory nodded. "Right. Building the population."

Alandriel took her to the mother–baby clinic. Exam rooms lined the first hall. A couple of women with big, round bellies passed them. They turned a corner and heard newborn cries. The pair donned masks, gowns, and gloves and entered the nursery. A few mothers in rockers held tiny humans to their breasts. Perfect little hands clasped their gowns. One mother saw the wonder in Rory's eyes and motioned for her to come closer. The baby hungrily suckled, and the girl held out the baby's arm. Rory placed a finger in the palm, and the baby held on. Rory adored it and decided to come back and volunteer more when she had time.

For now, her time was spent at the infirmary in the fortified CMO building. She and Jimena compiled computerized lists of the military branches and battles. They, with a few others, kept the information up to date. Some additional pockets of dragons were discovered, but they were sparse and spread out in thin numbers, so squadrons went out each day to meticulously pick the groups off.

Keeping the ledger became a full-time job. Men and women returned daily, and each soldier was checked in to the system as they entered the Briar. Rory and the others sat at a long metal table for hours on end. The task was made bearable by knowing their citizens were still alive. If one arrived with a flesh wound, Rory left her post to tend to it. Thankfully, they had only lost forty-four so far. Rory wanted the time of war to be over soon but dreaded the next few weeks, knowing the flight team would advance on the largest dragon colony.

In the fourth week, Alandriel entered the large hall excitedly, shouting, "The major general! He's returned!"

Rory's spirits lifted somewhat, knowing Jacoby was okay. He stormed in, holding a blood-soaked cloth against his forehead, followed by four of his men. They assured the crowd gathered that he would be all right and motioned for Rory to follow them into the procedure room.

She ran close behind. Jacoby sat on the examination table and ordered everyone except Rory to leave the room. The men paused to make sure of what he said.

"Leave now," he roared.

His grumpiness made Rory a little nervous, but she dared not show it.

"Lock the door," he ordered.

She obeyed, not looking at his face.

He spoke more quietly. "It's not that bad. Just put some stitches in."

Rory let out an audible sigh as she laid out instruments and dressings. She didn't care if he noticed. She hated being alone with him in that moment. Her body responded to his presence. She set up a separate tray with warm water and a towel to clean the blood from his hair and face. She wheeled it over to him, feeling her cheeks burn. She looked into his eyes and saw the look of pain and regret. She couldn't help but smile a little. She had missed him so. Seeing her smile, his lips curled up at the corners.

"Jake, does it hurt much?"

"If you're referring to my head, no," he replied softly.

She knew exactly what he was not saying. He closed his eyes when she began wiping the rag over his face. He felt her pulsing vibrations. Experiencing the sensation again brought him instant calm. It also created a renewed sadness. She belonged to another. He had lost her to Quinn.

The blood was gone, and she switched out the dirty tray for a sterile one. When her back was turned, he pulled off his bloody shirt and threw it on top of the pile of soiled towels. She felt shaken by his sudden lack of clothing. He stayed upright so the bleeding wouldn't increase. This left her only the choice of sliding between his knees to sew up the gash.

She sensed his heart pounding. It matched hers thudding in her own ears. It took everything in her being to steady her hands. Rory was ashamed to have this reaction. She picked up a full syringe of numbing medicine.

"This will only sting like a wasp for about ten seconds."

With the first push, Jacoby sucked in a deep breath, and as a natural reflex his left hand grabbed her waist, his fingers digging in. She nearly jumped but swallowed back a response and restrained herself. His right hand balled into a fist. He didn't let go. He drew her energy into his system. He'd been without for too long. Rory knew he was getting a fix.

She sewed as fast as she could and placed a thin line of antibiotic ointment over the stitches. She instructed him on how to take care of it, attempting to keep it professional. His grip relaxed, and he looked at her but didn't break the bond. His pupils were dilated from the exchange. His drowsy look made him all the more attractive.

Rory pulled off the blue gloves and threw them on the tray. His hands latched onto hers like vices, pulling them up to his cheeks. He closed his eyes, stealing a few more moments with her. She relented and rubbed her thumbs over his thick eyebrows, soothing him.

Rory knew he would be the major general when he walked out of the room, but for now he was her Jake.

He looked in her eyes and sighed. "Thank you. I'm sorry we keep doing this."

"Hush. I told you to come to me. It helps you. It's okay. You need to get back now."

This time she was the one leaving him alone.

CHAPTER NINE

Seeing Jacoby made Rory miss Quinn all the more. After the remaining squadrons had been accounted for, they rested and went back out. Jake had already left again as well. Rory now had more free time and decided to go back to the brick yard with Alandriel to keep busy with something a little less stressful.

The mood at the mother–baby clinic felt different this time. A visibly upset doctor and two assistants stomped down the delivery hall out to the newborn wing. They paused in front of the nursery, pointed toward someone, and moved on.

Alandriel and Rory slowly went in after they were out of sight. The mood was quiet and somber. A tired mother sat feeding a grunting baby. She smiled as he got his fill and pulled him away.

"You want to hold him? He was orphaned this morning and I have my own to take care of."

She swaddled him and passed him over. Rory adored the warm squirming being in her arms. He had a lovely smell and the softest full head of dark hair.

"What's his name?"

"Oh, dear. The mother didn't make it long enough, but he was given his father's name. This one was supposed to be special, and he may still be, but we don't have many volunteers to take a newborn. He is a junior. His name is Jacoby."

Alandriel saw the shock on Rory's face. Rory's heart swelled, and she began to cry. She hugged him against her chest. The baby fell fast asleep, and Rory reluctantly placed him in a bassinet alongside other snoozing newborns. She didn't want to leave him.

Alandriel watched her watch little Jacoby. She whispered, "Rory, I know the nurses would let you come and help take care of him, if you want."

"Oh, I do. Badly. I could be here as much as possible. It couldn't hurt for him to have someone he could become familiar with. Someone to love him. It might help me while I'm without Quinn. I need to talk to him about it first."

"I mean, I could even come spend some time with him. He is lovely, and I'm sure if Jacoby knew what happened to the mother, he wouldn't want his son without the best care." Alandriel smiled.

"You mean the major general doesn't know?"

"He may, but I doubt it. It only just happened this morning, and the leaders let the women do all the work until the children are at least eleven or twelve."

"Do you think he has more kids?"

"I bet not. He was gone with bounty hunting missions after the wars. He was back for about a month before he left again. So, yes. That had to be about seven or eight more months he spent away and then ... well, you know. You saved him. In that one month, he probably visited the mother often. That's how it works to ensure fertilization results in pregnancy."

"Gosh, it sounds so scientific. If this is the major general's first child, I'm sure he would want to know."

"I will ask before we leave. Then you can contact him and speak with Quinn about it."

❖❖❖❖❖

Alandriel went to her place when they got back to the city. Rory sat alone in the apartment. It was too quiet.

Her thoughts were on the baby, and she missed Quinn so much. He had promised to call her when he got settled at the base after flight tests. She made herself get up and turn on some orchestral music. She wasn't hungry but heated up some soup and drank two glasses of wine, which eased her nerves a bit.

She jumped when her communicator beeped.

"Quinn?"

"Uh, no. It's Jake. Quinn should be calling shortly. He was briefing the flight team and then heading to a bunk for the night."

"Oh. I'm sorry. I'm a little on edge. So, you all are still making it okay?"

"Yes. I wanted to ask you about the brick yard."

Her heart skipped a beat. She didn't know if he would be upset with her. "Okay."

"I heard from one of the doctors. A woman ... um ..."

"I know. I guess you heard I was there today. Jake, I had no idea. I promise. Alandriel and I wanted to focus on other things. We walked around the clinic and went to the nursery and there was this beautiful little baby, and a woman practically handed him over, and he was the sweetest little thing ..."

"Rory. Stop. I'm not mad. Do you think I'm mad at you? I was informed the mother passed away after childbirth. I'm glad you got to see him. I bet he's cute."

"Oh, Jake, he is. He was so warm and snuggly, and I didn't want to leave him. He fell asleep in my arms. The mother who fed him called him an orphan, and I couldn't bear it. I was going to talk to Quinn first and then you, but I would like to get your permission to go see him again. As much as I can, if Quinn agrees, of course."

"I can't say no, now can I? It would mean the world to me. Let me know if Quinn has a problem with it. I don't think he will."

"Thank you. I'll go see him tomorrow morning if Quinn agrees. Thank you, Jake."

"All right. I'll talk to you soon. Good night."

Rory felt relief. One down. Her heart hoped Quinn would be as easily persuaded. A third glass of wine should help.

She would never get used to the beeping. "Hello, my husband," she said seductively.

"Rory, darling. I miss you too much. I wish you were here to warm up my bed for me ... and ... I can think of a few other things we could do."

"Believe me. I long for the same. It's so quiet in our apartment. I think I'll leave the music going forever."

"And think of me dancing with you. Smelling you. Loving you."

"Quinn, I don't know if I can do this. Gosh, it's hard."

"I know, my love. You know, this is the first time I've been away that I've had someone to come home to, and, shit, it feels good."

"Quinn, I have something I wanted to talk to you about. I want to know how you honestly feel about it."

"Okay ... you know I'll tell you the truth."

"Alandriel and I visited the babies at the brick yard again today. There was an orphan there. The mother died after childbirth, and another woman with a new baby of her own was feeding him. She let me hold him and I ... I don't know. I felt like he needed me. I want to go back when I can and help the nurses care for him, but I wanted to tell you and I need to tell you more about him."

"Well, what is it? Is he sick? You know I wouldn't mind you loving a baby. I'm sure it's impossible not to."

"He's perfect and healthy. He's ... it's just ... he's Jacoby's son."

"Ah ..."

"I had no idea when I held him. I was shocked when the other mother told me."

"Does Jake know?"

"I was going to talk to you first, but he called me just before you did. He sounded sad about the mother but happy he has a son. He would be grateful if I visited the baby, but I told him it would be up to you. You are my number one. I never want you to be second or to feel anything negative about us."

"If it makes you happy, I want you to do it. I could never deny you any sort of happiness in life. You are my everything, and I know you can't have a baby of your own. I think you might be very good for the little thing. He might be good for you, too, since I'll be gone for a while. I love your heart, Rory."

"I love you. Thank you. I hate that I won't be able to talk to you after the next couple of days."

"I promise to call you tomorrow at lunch. We can talk longer. Tonight won't be the same without you. I love you. Try to sleep well."

❊❊❊❊❊❊

Rory woke with a purpose. She couldn't wait to see that little bundle of joy. She stopped at the mercantile first to buy newborn clothes, blankets, and a stuffed animal. She wanted him to have things that belonged to him.

The doctor had arranged for little Jacoby to have his own room, per the major general's wishes. It was perfectly complete, with a fancy baby bed and an airship mobile twirling overhead, and smelled of baby powder. A nurse had just finished changing his diaper when Rory came in, and she handed him over with a smile.

"Oh, thank you. Hello, little man. Hello, my sweet. I missed you. Oh, ma'am, I wanted to know if it's okay if we just call him Jay for now?"

"Yes, ma'am. Whatever you want. The major general is very thankful you volunteered to be a caregiver. He said we can trust you with any decisions."

"Oh. Thank you. Yes. Please, call me any time when I'm not here if you need anything."

Jay cooed, and Rory sat in a blue plush rocker, holding him on her shoulder. His nose was near her cheek, and she felt his breath. Yes. She could get used to this. The nurse helped her change a diaper for the first time and told her a bath would be tomorrow.

Rory read a book while Jay went to feed with the surrogate, and Quinn called.

"Hi, stranger. I miss you."

"How's it going today? You loving on that baby?"

"Oh, Quinn. He's so sweet. I changed my first diaper today." She laughed.

"I guess I've never changed one. I like picturing you holding a baby. I bet you look lovely."

"I wish you could see him. Maybe I can get a photo delivered to you soon."

"Yes. I'd love that. You should send one to Jacoby too. I've noticed him holding his head a little higher and smiling more now that he knows he has a son. It's good for him."

"I'm glad. The colony needs him to be strong. Especially now."

"I'll be able to call tomorrow, but then I will be unable to contact you until after the first airstrike. Everything is looking good. I need to get back. I love you. I think about you constantly."

"Love you too. Can't wait to hear from you tomorrow."

❄❄❄❄❄❄

When Rory arrived at the brick yard the next day, a nurse had Jay up, fed, and dressed. She informed Rory that the major general had arranged for a funeral to honor the mother of his child, and he wished Rory would attend in his absence.

"Of course."

A small graveyard surrounded by a beautiful garden sat inside the wall behind the mother–baby clinic, and there were a handful of people gathered around the shiny silver coffin. A familiar nurse had a guitar and played old hymns Rory had heard before at the Crossroads. A soft wind blew through the trees lining the brick wall, and the sun shined warm and bright as she joined the strangers. The eulogy was short. The other mourners left before the coffin descended underground. Rory plucked a velvety, red rose from one of the nearby bushes and tossed it on top before the vault was sealed. When she returned to Jay, she held him close, thankful that his life was spared.

She spoke to Quinn again at lunch, and he promised to call as soon as the flight team was safely back at the base.

⁂⁂⁂⁂⁂

Rory went to bed very early but tossed and turned, thinking about the first mission to be executed before sunrise the next day. After two hours, she got up and ate a few nettie berries from her pantry. She lay back down but then got a call.

"Rory?"

"Jake?"

"Hi. Is it too late?"

"No. No. I couldn't sleep. I'm nervous, you know?"

"Yes. I know. Me too." They laughed a little.

"I wanted to thank you for going to the funeral today. It means a lot."

"Oh yeah. It was nice. That was nice of you to do that."

"It feels good to know I had a hand in creating life. I have someone to live for, you know? I mean, I'll always defend the colony and ... you. I won't lie. I get through sometimes thinking of you. Anyway, I'm sorry."

"It's okay. You're just being honest, and I appreciate it, but yes! I can't wait for you and Quinn to meet him. I'm calling him Jay, if that's okay?"

"Yes. I love it. All right. I better go. Kiss Jay for me."

A very long week followed. Rory spent time with Jay, and Alandriel visited often. They were together at the brick yard when they got word the flight team had returned to base. The mother–baby clinic had a television screen that only streamed news.

They went to the lobby to see for themselves. A newswoman reported on the success, and they could see Quinn and Dex in the background with the other airmen and women in celebration. Rory and Alandriel beamed at each other with relief.

The newswoman spoke to Quinn. "Captain Barton, did you expect such an easy win?"

"Oh, well, no, ma'am. You never know how these things will turn out, but we did a lot of planning and had a solid strategy in place. The ground troops are moving in as we speak. We anticipate an end to this conflict very soon and then we will be scouting a bit further to ensure the danger has passed."

He looked into the recorder, winked, and blew a kiss with the biggest smile. Rory swooned and finally took a breath. Alandriel grasped onto her, and they cried a few happy tears.

The call she was waiting on finally came when she was back at home.

"Rory Barton, I'm coming home to you."

"Seriously? Oh, Quinn."

"All of us airmen and women are returning for a little bit before we have to go out scouting again. None of us want to wait, so we're heading there now. I should be home in the morning."

"Oh my gosh. You don't know how happy I am right now. I hope I can sleep. Should I meet you at the CMO?"

"No. It will be early. Just stay in bed, and I'll join you in a few hours," he laughed.

"Can't wait."

❄❄❄❄❄❄

Quinn slid under the covers, and Rory turned over to be wrapped up by him. She vibrated, and he moaned. He smelled her hair as she kissed his bare chest.

"I missed you, darling. I live for this."

She scooted up a bit to kiss his mouth. Her mouth. She loved the fact that he was hers. His heart. His body. She ran her hands all over him, and he rolled on top.

He just wanted to look at her for a moment. She adjusted her legs around his waist, and he entered her. They made slow, sweet love to each other, savoring every movement, touch, and kiss.

Then they took a shower together, had breakfast, and cuddled on the couch for a while. They couldn't get enough contact.

"We should go see that baby."

"We should. You'll fall in love, Quinn."

❄❄❄❄❄❄

It was mid-morning, and Rory was surprised to see Jimena rocking Jay.

"Oh, hi! I hope you don't mind. I knew you and Alandriel would be spending time with Dex and the captain, so I figured I'd come see the little guy."

"No, I don't mind at all. I appreciate it. You can come any time. This little one has more friends than he realizes."

Rory smoothed a hand over his head, and Jimena kissed him before turning him over. The women stared at Quinn's face. He didn't blink. His eyes were misty.

"You weren't kidding. I totally get why you fell under his spell." Quinn took him and smelled his hair. He rocked him in his arms and kissed the soft spot atop his head. "How do you ever leave him?"

"I told you it's hard, but the nurses are lovely with him. He is important. I have to remind myself that."

Jimena stepped out as Quinn and Rory oohed and aahed over him. Quinn gave Jay back and took out his military-issued communicator. It had a camera and recorder, and he took a picture.

"You know, Jacoby needs to meet him."

Rory sat down in the rocker and laid him on her lap.

"Here, take one without me in it. For Jake."

"Have you talked to him?"

She hesitated. "Yes. He only called to ask about Jay and how the funeral went for the mother. He arranged a small service and burial here in the brick yard. It was nice. I went for him."

"Oh good. That was very thoughtful. I can't imagine. He should be here in a few days. It'll do him some good to see his son."

"Does this make you want a son? I want to know the truth. You could have a child the way Jake did, couldn't you?"

"Rory! No. just ... no. I would never." He kneeled down at her knees and looked down at Jay. "You are all I need. All I want. I don't need anything or anyone else. I keep thinking about how you must feel, though. Do you wish you had a baby of your own?"

"I never did before. I have had a moment or two of sadness, knowing I just can't, but it was fleeting. This is my life and I can't ask for more. I think I could volunteer here and be happy with that."

"And I'm sure Jacoby will let you keep this precious boy close."

Jay clamped onto his finger. Rory smiled.

"It's time for him to feed. He's being weened to take bottles. We can go. I can check on the library on the way home."

While she put a few books back on shelves, Quinn paced back and forth outside on the sidewalk. He appeared fairly stressed, talking into his communicator. He made her nervous, and his face didn't comfort her when he walked inside.

"What? What happened?"

"It's okay. My team took care of most of the dragons, and the ground troops are more than capable of handling the stragglers, but the first line was met by a couple of buried mines. There may not be any fatalities at all since tanks drove out before the foot soldiers, but there are injuries. A cargo plane full of patients is on its way. We should get to the infirmary."

Alandriel and Dex had beat them there. Rory took a seat beside Jimena. New information came in—there were extensive wounds which required several soldiers be sent straight to the hospital, where surgeons waited ready for emergencies.

Quinn and Dex disappeared for a while to meet with Colonel Lewis and Jacoby, who had been to the hospital first to assess the situation there. A news crew arrived, and everyone at the CMO was directed to go to the auditorium for a briefing. The military leaders and members of the council sat in chairs on stage. Jacoby commanded the podium.

"Good afternoon. Um, as you have all heard by now, there was an incident this morning well beyond our safe zone. It did not involve dragon soldiers. Only mines, which were not detected until it was too late. As of right now, multiple injuries were sustained, but no fatalities. We have highly qualified surgeons,

specialists, and nurses working to ensure the best outcome for our men and women. We thank them for their
bravery, and we thank you, the citizens of the Briar, for
your ongoing support. We will contact affected family
members as soon as possible."

Jacoby looked right at Rory. She smiled and nodded,
letting him know he had done well. He exited behind
the stage door.

Quinn trotted down the steps off the stage to Rory.
"We'll be all right. I'm starving. Let's go home for
dinner."

Jacoby headed straight for the brick yard. He felt a
primal need to meet his son. Everyone at the mother–
baby clinic was surprised to see him so soon after his
return. He spoke with the doctor who had delivered
Jay—Dr. Theo Todd, who was also head of the council—and a nurse showed him to the baby's room.

It was soothing. He walked in quietly and looked into
the crib. Little Jay lay awake, bright eyes staring up at
the mobile. He cooed when he saw Jacoby and kicked
his feet out from under his blanket. Jacoby laughed and
reached in, smoothing his dark, feather-soft hair. When
Jay grinned, Jacoby scooped him up and held him up to
his shoulder. He swayed back and forth, and the baby
seemed to enjoy it, making sounds Jacoby had never
heard before. He sat in the rocker, feeling at complete
peace. Before he knew it, they both fell fast asleep.

❊❊❊❊❊❊❊

Rory arrived early to the brick yard. She loved giving
Jay his morning bath and was in high spirits having
Quinn home. A nurse stopped Rory in the hall before
she went into the room. She pointed, grinning. When
Rory peeped in, she saw the sweetest sight. Jacoby and
Jay were still asleep. Jake snored, but it didn't wake
the baby. Rory decided not to bother them and went to

the nursery to help with the other babies for the morning.

Rory scurried by Jay's door later, and Jacoby wasn't around. She went in and heard beautiful music playing on a radio she guessed his father had gifted him. He was twisting and giggling in his crib. She picked him up and bounced him a bit, kissing his head.

Jacoby returned and saw Rory dancing around with Jay. He fell in love all over again. She felt his eyes on her and turned around, glowing.

"Oh, hi. I didn't want to bother you two earlier, but when you weren't here, I let myself in. The music is lovely."

He came to stand next to them, gently touching the baby's toes. "He seems to like it. I think he's smitten with you."

"Well, the feeling is mutual."

"I can't ever thank you enough for taking all of this on. You didn't have to, and I know it's a strange situation ..."

"I feel like I was meant to. I loved him as soon as I held him. I had no idea who he was or that his mom didn't make it, but I loved him."

Jacoby's hand instinctively touched her back as she spoke, but he jerked it away when a nurse walked in to bring bottles. She left, and he put a little space between them. He respected Quinn enough not to act on his feelings. Rory gave little Jay back over so Jacoby could sit with him. She handed him a bottle, and he touched the nipple to the baby's lips. Jay welcomed it and sucked down the entire thing.

"Wow, you hungry little creature. You are a good boy. Yes, you are," he baby-talked.

Rory looked around and found Jacoby's communicator on the dresser. She grabbed it and took a picture of father and son. Jacoby heard the click and looked up with the biggest smile as she took another.

Little Jay fell asleep soon after taking his bottle. Jacoby went home to sleep in in his own bed, and Rory went home to Quinn.

❊❊❊❊❊❊

She walked into the apartment to dinner, hot and ready. She slid her shoes off, and Quinn fed her a meatball with a fork.

"Mmm. So good, Quinn."

"I've missed cooking. The food at the base can't compare."

"I've missed your cooking too." She laughed.

"I noticed all of the soup in the fridge."

She laughed again. "I don't go hungry." Rory went up on her tiptoes and kissed his cheek.

They sat and enjoyed being together again. When the kitchen was clean, the pair curled up close on the couch and listened to their favorite music as it floated through the air.

CHAPTER TEN

An end was in sight. Miles and miles of territory had been cleared. The bodies of dragons were buried. Colonel Lewis suggested Quinn make one more trip out to fly his airship to the farthest perimeter, since it was an almost totally silent craft. If they left at dusk, it would be difficult to be seen in the clouds. Jacoby fell back into bounty hunter mode and insisted he come along. He would take Toby to search any caves or hillside dwellings they might come across, and he ordered that a platoon accompany the mission.

Rory stood between Jacoby and Quinn as they watched men and women load supplies onto the airship and four tanks. She slid her arm in the crook of Jacoby's and took the photo of little Jay from her bag to give him. He kissed it and tucked it in his pocket. He hugged her, then walked toward the airship.

Rory took out the other picture of herself holding Jay and placed it in the pocket over Quinn's heart. He wrapped her up, lifting her off her feet.

"We will be waiting for you."

"I'm counting the seconds. Kiss me, darling."

She did. She couldn't let go. Her hands stayed in his hair as he set her back down.

"I could come with you."

"No, darling. You have someone here who needs you. I'll call you soon." He kissed her deeply one more time. "My heart stays here."

❊❊❊❊❊❊

The Lark floated silently through a starry sky. Quinn had named his ship the Lark after he and Rory married.

The platoon scouted a half-mile behind the Lark at all times. When the airship grounded during daylight hours, the tanks stopped too.

On the third night, Quinn could tell they were approaching a body of water. Light fog crept over the ground. The Lark floated above the haze. Jacoby had retired to his cabin to rest. Quinn slept during the day so he could fly all night. Colonel Lewis sat in the copilot chair and snoozed.

Quinn slowed the ship a bit. He caught a glimpse of a red light. Only a flicker. He watched intently to see if it repeated ... again a short, red flash.

"Oh shit."

"What? What is it?" the colonel grumbled.

"Oh shit! Oh shit! There!"

Colonel Lewis sat forward to see the red light flashing faster now.

"Go get Jake!"

Colonel Lewis ran from the helm toward the sleeping cabins. Quinn quickly tried to put the Lark in reverse. He grabbed the communicator while he feverishly flipped switches.

"Red! Code red! The Lark is under threat. I repeat. The Lark is under threat."

"Roger that. We're on our way."

The platoon accelerated their advance and located the Lark. They pulled forward as the airship reversed.

Quinn dropped the communicator and braced himself when he saw a large burst of light in the distance trailed by a recognizable tail. A rocket smashed into the bottom corner of the hull. Flames licked the sides of the ship. Jacoby and Colonel Lewis felt the impact of the rocket, and the Lark faltered. They had to stop where they were in the middle of the ship to brace for another possible impact. The Lark was going down. They heard the sounds of tanks firing back.

There was nothing Quinn could do. The dashboard lights went crazy, shorting out. He smelled smoke from burning wires as sparks flew, and he slid down to the floor to crawl toward the door to the flight deck. He felt a sudden drop in altitude, and the hull crashed into the ground nose first, crumpling the walls around him. The helm was wrecked, and Quinn lay trapped under debris, so close to the exit. He could hardly catch a breath—the pain in his legs was unbearable. He heard shouting and banging on the splintered door. It cracked as Jacoby and Colonel Lewis ripped pieces off. Once cleared, they found Quinn, only free from mid-chest up. He struggled to make space to breathe, and fire now burned the dashboard. They needed to get him out fast. The men pushed, pulled, and forced enough out of the way to drag him out.

"My legs! They're broken for sure," he cried.

Jacoby noticed blood. Lots of it, emptying from the inside of Quinn's thigh, soaking the fabric of his own pants as he kneeled by his side. He tore off his uniform shirt and tied the sleeve up around the other man's groin. Quinn's breathing became faster and labored. Tears rolled down his face.

"He's got a punctured lung," the colonel stated.

Quinn's shaking hand fumbled around for his pocket and pulled out the photo of Rory and Jay. He closed Jacoby's hand around it.

"Tell them ... I love them."

"Quinn. No. Stop! I'll get you back. I'll drag you home if I have to." Jacoby cried, "Rory needs you."

"You may get me back, but ... we both know ... I won't be seeing them. Promise. Promise me ... you'll go to her. Don't leave her alone. I don't care ... what duty calls for. You do what's right, Jake."

Jacoby turned to the colonel, who only shook his head with a sad, knowing look. Quinn sucked in a breath, and his eyelids fluttered.

Jacoby leaned down to his ear, tears rolling down his own face. "You are the best man, Quinn. You were what Rory needed. She is your light. You carry her with you."

Quinn's body suddenly relaxed. His chin fell to his shoulder, and he was gone. Jacoby wept over him. He had just lost a friend and colleague, but Rory had lost far more.

Colonel Lewis, with tears in his own eyes, grabbed his arm. "We have to get out of here."

Jacoby hoisted Quinn's limp body over his shoulder, and the men trudged their way down the flight deck. Soldiers from the platoon were waiting at the bottom.

"Someone wrap him in fresh blankets. I have to go see Toby."

"Major general, surely you don't think he made it?" the colonel questioned.

Jacoby ignored him and kept walking to the rear of the burning craft. Gray smoke billowed up in the black night sky. The raging fire hadn't reached the equine hold, but there were no sounds coming from the stall as Jacoby neared the door. He cracked it open. Toby didn't move. He lay on the hay with no signs of life. Jacoby fell on his stained knees beside the stallion and broke down again. Feeling the heat of the ever-nearing blaze, he patted the horse's flank and let him be. He left the hold and paced back to his men.

"What do you want to do with the horse?" the colonel asked.

"Leave him. Let him burn with the Lark."

A soldier handed Jacoby a uniform not covered in blood.

"Do we know what exactly happened out there?"

Another soldier stepped forward. "Yes, sir. It was a small company. Only three dragons. They used their own type of Atlas AT4. We easily took them out with a HEAT round. All seems quiet now."

"All right ... let's keep two tanks out here for another twenty-four hours to make sure we don't have any more surprises. The rest of us will take Quinn—Captain Barton back to the Briar. I have to call his wife."

❊❊❊❊❊

Jacoby sat on the edge of a hard mattress on an even harder metal bunk in one of the tanks. He flipped the communicator over in his hand, trying to figure out what to say to Rory. He didn't want to give her this news with a call. He checked the time. It was nearing sunrise. He decided to call the CMO and have a mass message go out to the family members of the participating soldiers to meet in the CMO auditorium at 10 a.m. He gave strict instructions not to alert the media or any other citizens.

Before the light of day touched the earth, Rory heard a beep signaling a new message. The words were so vague. No hint of victory in them. She didn't have a good feeling. She sat on the bed for a while, unsettled and numb. Something inside her was off. Almost like she was in a dream state. Not sure what propelled her, she went to Quinn's closet. Her hand ran along the hanging clothes. She pulled a white T-shirt from his drawer and smelled it ... and began to weep. Her intuition whispered to her heart, and she prepared herself to hear the worst.

Rory asked Alandriel and Dex to meet her at the CMO. The Lark was nowhere in sight in the airfield next to the building. The trio walked into the large hall as people filtered into the auditorium.

Jacoby peered around the steel door to see if she had arrived. When their eyes met, his mouth set in a straight line, his face apologetic. Hot tears formed in her eyes as he stalked over to her, grabbed her wrist, and pulled her away from the others.

"I knew it. I just knew it. I felt it. I ..."

He held her as she fell to pieces. He cried with her. It hurt him to have to explain. "Rory ... the Lark was hit. It went down. Quinn was in the front, and he got trapped. There was too much debris. He knew he wasn't going to make it. I'm sorry. I'm so sorry. He gave me this."

He pulled back enough to hand her the picture. Rory sighed. She turned it over. On the back, Quinn had written,

My heart stays here.

"His thoughts were of you and little Jay. He told me to tell you how much he loved you both."

Her heart crumbled again. This loss hit far deeper than when she had lost Shaw.

"I don't ... I don't know what to do. Where is he? Is he here?"

"Of course. He will have a proper military burial in a few days. Rory, I'll be right beside you."

Rory wiped her face, straightened her clothes, and smoothed her hair. "I don't want to go to the briefing. I can't."

"You don't have to. Everyone will understand."

"Can I just go see Jay?"

"Can I meet you there after all of this?"

"Yes, please."

He took her hands but felt no heat or vibrations. He looked down at them and then at her face, questioning.

"I'm just ... numb."

"We'll get through this."

※※※※※※

Rory went straight to the brick yard. She couldn't go home and see Quinn's things yet. She could hardly believe what was now her reality. Her heart hurt. Her spirit was crushed. Rory held everything in until she stepped into Jay's room, closing the door behind her.

Then tears flowed freely. She saw him sleeping and sank to the floor. She took out the picture Jacoby had returned to her and rubbed her fingers over the words on the back.

She whispered, "My love. My Quinn. Why did you have to leave me? I can't do this without you. What am I to do now?"

Jay cooed. Rory dried her face and pulled herself together. She picked him up and held him close. He laughed, and she turned on the radio, dancing around the room as best as she could.

"I still have you now, don't I? Are you my best little friend? Yes, you are."

Alandriel walked in and started to cry.

"Oh, Rory. I'm so sorry. I can't believe it."

"Hush. I'll start again. I can't believe it either. I don't know what I'm going to do."

Alandriel sighed. "D is torn up too. We all are. I even saw the major general crying today, but he didn't see me."

"I know I'll probably be here a lot and at the library to keep busy. Alandriel, I don't want to go home."

A deep voice chimed in—Jacoby stood in the doorway. "I'll take you home. See how you feel. If it's too much, we'll get some of your things and get you the best suite at the Crown."

Rory looked away.

"That's where they spent their honeymoon."

"Oh, I didn't know. I'm sorry ... oh, the governor's house. It's finished and furnished, sitting empty right now."

"That's too nice of you. I'll think about it. I'll see how I feel."

She handed Jay to his father.

The proud new dad beamed. "He's a handsome devil, isn't he?"

Alandriel hugged Rory hard. "If you need anything, I mean anything, call me. I love you."

Jacoby sat in the rocker with Jay, and Rory paced around the room, humming to the music. The baby got fussy, and she made him a bottle. She liked watching Jacoby feed him. She had a memory of Jake and the affection he had showed Toby at the Crossroads.

"Toby!"

"He didn't make it. I just let him burn with the Lark."

"I'm sorry, Jake."

"No. Don't say that. That's nothing compared to what you lost."

Jay finished, and Rory showed Jacoby how to burp him.

"Know what's next?"

"Judging by the warm heaviness I'm feeling, diaper change?"

Rory did it while Jacoby watched. "Next time, you can give it a try."

"You know, I could pull rank ..."

She laughed. "Yes, I guess you could. What are your plans for him?"

"I'd rather not leave him here much longer. There are lots of rooms at the governor's house."

"Yes. It looks like a mansion from the outside."

"I guess it sort of is. We should let this little guy nap. He's yawning. You ready to head over to your apartment?"

They sat in silence in a booth on the train along with two armed guards. Rory thought of that first passionate night with Quinn and how he was completely hers. And now he wasn't. She felt utterly depressed.

Once in her apartment, Rory remained quiet. Jacoby didn't say a word as he watched her float around the room, touching every surface. He reached for wine from the fridge and presented two glasses.

"May I?"

"Yes, of course. Might help."

Jacoby sat on a stool, and Rory leaned on the counter.

"You know, he was my angel. I know how he behaved before, but he was everything good for me."

"You did it, Rory. It was all you. You gave him the world and he adored you. I'll admit. I have had a tough time. You noticed, too. Anger, jealousy, depression. The thing is, I knew it didn't matter. You and Quinn were exactly where you were supposed to be. Everyone saw the change in him. That makes this all the more tragic. I knew you were happy, and I wanted you to be happy for the rest of your life, even if it wasn't with me."

Rory poured more wine. "I can't stay here. I can't sleep in our bed without him."

"Go. Take your time. Get whatever you need. You're staying at the mansion tonight."

"Will I be alone in that huge house?"

"The staff is there. There are so many rooms. It's ridiculous. I'll have groceries delivered this afternoon."

"Just give me a few moments." Rory entered the bedroom and closed the door. She went to Quinn's closet and clung to his clothes. She cried again. She packed a couple of his T-shirts with her things and got his apron from the kitchen. She adored watching him cook in that apron.

"Anything else?" He saw her eyeing the radio and retrieved it.

"Thank you, Jake."

$$\maltese\maltese\maltese\maltese$$

The long black car pulled through the iron gate. The house looked somewhat like a fancy hotel or government building but without being cold. Another car already sat in front of the big steps, where Alandriel took her bag from the back seat.

"While you were packing, I called her to keep you company the first night here. I hope that's okay?"

"Yes. Thank you." Rory hugged her friend hard.

"Wow! This is lovely. I've been watching the progress as they built it, but never thought I'd be spending the night."

Jacoby carried their bags up the steps, and a butler opened the door. "This is Vincent. He will give you a proper tour."

"I'll be right back, Alandriel."

She walked out with Jacoby, and he leaned against the car.

"I'll come by to discuss the service." He reached out and touched her arm. "Please try and get some sleep."

She stepped into his embrace, and he smoothed her hair. "Thank you for everything."

He kissed her forehead and let go, then she walked back to the front door.

"Ladies, may I take your things?"

They followed Vincent up a gorgeous black wooden staircase to a long hall covered in embossed navy wallpaper with black doors on each side. Rory ran her hand along the surface of the wall, admiring its extravagance. Their rooms were next to each other.

"Our decorator chose a gothic Victorian aesthetic. You each have a washroom. We will go back down through the formal parlor to the kitchen. There is a ballroom with a guest wing on the other side of the mansion."

Rory paused at the door at the top of the steps. It was open, and she saw a beautiful, masculine office with a large carved desk, bookshelves, and a stone fireplace.

"That will be Governor Garrick's study."

The parlor looked more modern, with painted walls the color of an eggshell, an enormous white marble-tiled fireplace, and four thick-button-tufted couches the color of a blue sky. Potted plants sat in the corners, giving the room a lush, alive feeling. A woman prepared sandwiches in the huge restaurant-style kitchen. It reminded her she hadn't eaten since the day before. The woman set a glass-top table and left the two friends alone.

"It still doesn't feel real. Feels like I'm starting all over again."

"I'm so sorry. I can't say that I know how you feel at all. I know how much you and Quinn loved each other. D and I want a love like that. I know you were everything to him."

Vincent returned to take up the empty plates. Rory's communicator beeped.

"Oh, hi, Jimena. Thank you for thinking of me. What are you doing tonight? Want to spend the night in the governor's mansion?"

After Jimena arrived and the others gave her a tour, the three took ice cream to Rory's room, put on pajamas, and turned on the radio.

"It's awfully nice of the major general to let us stay here. I heard at the CMO that the council wants to swear him in as soon as next week," Jimena said.

Alandriel licked her spoon. "They should. I don't know why they waited so long."

"Quinn told me they wanted to do it when it could really be celebrated. Like, the Briar would enter a new era. A bigger, even better one, when the threat of war wasn't on the minds of the citizens. Keeps the morale up and everyone happy."

Rory went down to dispose of the trash and got another call.

"Rory."

"Hi, Jake."

"You settled? Are you okay? Need anything?"

"We're good. I hope it's okay Jimena joined us."

"Yes, of course. Did you eat?"

"Yes, sir. We just finished the delicious peppermint ice cream you sent."

"Oh yeah. It's my favorite. Listen, you all have the run of the house. Make yourselves at home."

"Thank you, but I think we will keep to our rooms. We are all pretty emotionally drained. I brought my nettie berries to help me sleep."

"Good. Good. I'll be by early in the morning. Good night."

❊❊❊❊❊

Rory woke up with the sun and shed a few more tears over being without Quinn. She hugged a pillow close and spoke to him like he was lying beside her. "Quinn, my love. What am I to do? Help me. Tell me how I should go on. I miss you so. Please, wherever you are ... know that I love you."

She had a long shower, as did the other girls, then followed the smell of bacon and eggs downstairs.

"You need us to stay longer?" Alandriel asked.

"I don't think so. I'll manage. I plan on seeing Jay today and then I may go find a book in the study and read for a bit."

Jacoby walked in with a bouquet of dark red roses, and Vincent put them in a vase. Jacoby sat next to Rory at the table and spoke softly.

"Lieutenant Baxter told me you used these at your wedding ceremony. I thought they would be nice for the service."

Rory wiped a tear away. "Yes. They are perfect. I have a couple of ideas of what he would have liked."

"Of course. You were his wife. I'll make sure we honor Quinn and what he would want."

Alandriel and Jimena had never seen the major general look at anyone the way he looked at Rory. His smile and gentle demeanor surprised them. They could tell he cared for her a great deal. They stood up from the table.

"We will get our things. We can stop by the library for a bit."

Jacoby stood. "Thank you both for staying."

Rory added, "Yes. I love you two."

Jacoby took Rory's hand and led her up to the study. She sat on the couch, and he took a notebook and pen from his desk and started to pull up the chair.

"Jake. Come sit here." She patted the cushion next to her, and they began to plan the perfect memorial that was to be held in two days.

Rory prepared herself to weep again. She tucked one of Quinn's handkerchiefs into the bodice of her black dress. Jacoby got ready across the hall in what would soon be his bedroom. She went to the study and watched out the window as three cars pulled up and parked on the street. Jacoby came in, looking amazing in his uniform. He carried his cape over one arm.

"Let me." She placed it over his shoulders, and he closed the clasp.

"Thank you. You look perfect. The weather is perfect. I'll be right behind you."

They walked out, and he helped her into the second car. Quinn's ashes rested in the first with Dex beside them. Jacoby got into the third.

A light breeze moved through the air as the procession ended at the city center. Uniformed guards lined almost the entire length of the pier, along with army and flight team members. Dark red roses twisted around the metal railings.

Dex carried the silver urn with white gloves, followed by Rory flanked by Alandriel and Jimena, then Jacoby. Drummers played a solemn, calm beat until they reached the end—the same place Quinn had watched her every night after work. The same place he had professed his love, and the same precious place Quinn and Rory had recited their vows. As the drumming halted, a single fighter airship flew across the water. A light breeze stirred again, and a violinist began a beautiful, sad melody. Dex tearfully passed the urn to Rory. She hugged it to her chest, kissed it, and whispered, "Your heart stays here."

She leaned over the edge and delicately scattered Quinn's ashes over the Lake of Peace. She pulled a single sentimental rose from the rail and tossed it in. Dex did the same, then Jacoby. The rest of the attendees followed suit. It was beautiful. The sun began to set. The crowd dispersed, and Jacoby touched her elbow.

"I want to stay for a little while."

"I'll see you at home. A car will wait for you." He motioned for the guards to follow so she could be alone.

Rory cried out everything she had left to give. She closed her eyes and felt a warm breath on the back of her neck. Just like Quinn's breath. It sent shivers through her being, and her hands vibrated on the metal rail. It surprised her, but she was relieved to have the sensation again.

She slowly made her way back to the car and asked the driver to wait a few minutes. She bought bread and two apple ciders.

Rory entered the huge house quietly when Vincent greeted her at the door. Only a few lamps were on, casting shadows around the large rooms. Jacoby sat up with his head reclined, asleep in his pajamas on one of the parlor couches. She knew he had tried to wait up for her. She sat beside him and held one of the cups under his nose, letting it waft warm cinnamon steam into his nostrils. He stirred, blinked, and smiled.

"Mmm. Cider. Thank you."

He took the cup for a sip. She opened the bag, showing him the rolls.

"Quinn and I had these at least twice a week. I'm sorry if it bothers you hearing about ..."

"No. I'm all ears."

"Thank you. Are you not going back to your place?"

"Well, actually, all my things will be transferred here next week. There is a big deal to be made, you know. A swearing-in, a ball ..."

"A ball? Wow. Wait. I shouldn't be here. The council ..."

"Screw the council. You're here. You're here as long as you like. I want you here. You must know that."

"I do," she said quietly. "You could tell them I'm a maid or a nanny." She laughed.

He grabbed her hand. "Rory. Don't."

Her hand vibrated, and his eyebrows raised.

"It's back?"

She nodded. "It's back."

"When?"

She looked down at his hand holding hers.

"I felt him. Quinn. When I was alone on the pier. I felt him say goodbye, say everything is going to be all right, and it came back."

He squeezed her hand. "Good. Now sleep. We'll go see Jay tomorrow."

CHAPTER ELEVEN

D r. Todd spoke with Jacoby while Rory changed Jay into an outfit she had brought.

"You know the boy has a bright future. Good genes. The son of the soon-to-be governor. Do you have plans to take him to the mansion?"

"That would be ideal."

"Would Ms. Rory be willing to stay on as caregiver?" Jacoby watched her loving on Jay.

Dr. Todd lowered his voice. "You have an heir now. There should be a way to persuade the council to accept such a union. I, as commissioner, am willing to give them my opinion of the situation." His eyes went to Rory. "They would allow almost anything to keep you as governor of the Briar."

Jacoby smiled, thinking of the possibilities as the doctor left them alone. "Rory, I'd like to take Jay home. What do you think?"

She lit up. "Today? That would be lovely. We could take him to play in the garden, and he would have so much room to run around when he gets going ... I mean, if you still want me to watch him."

"You know I do. I mean, he can't stay here. He's my son. I want him at home. We'll move everything to the room next to yours if you want. We won't have people around constantly."

"The council ..."

"Don't think about that now. I will ease them into it. They are busy with planning the ball and swearing-in ceremony."

Jacoby signed the release, and Rory watched a nurse pack up Jay's things. Then Jacoby led them around back to pay his respects to Jay's mother. Rory placed a rose on the grave, and they took Jay home.

A truck delivered everything to the mansion. Jacoby insisted on unloading it all himself. Rory spread a quilt on the parlor floor and played with Jay.

The door buzzed and Vincent answered the intercom. "Garrick residence. How may I help you?"

"Hello, it's Jimena. Is Rory there? May I come in for a few minutes?"

"Yes, Ms. Jimena. You may enter."

He pushed a button to open the gate, and she knocked on the door within a few minutes.

"Hi, Vincent! Oh, Rory! I'm so happy Jay is here. I went by the brick yard, but the nurse wasn't allowed to disclose any information."

"We've only been here a couple of hours. Jacoby is setting up his room."

The baby smiled and giggled at Jimena, and she picked him up.

"I'm going to check on the progress, if that's okay?"

"Sure. We'll be right here."

The room looked much like it had at the brick yard. Jacoby turned on the radio, and soft music played. Violin and cello were Rory's favorite. He took hold of her and swung her around the room.

"This is perfect. I'm going to love having him so close." Her eyes added, *and you.*

He paused with a hungry look, then let go.

"Let's show Jay."

❊❊❊❊❊

Rory got up during the night when Jay cried so Jacoby could sleep. He always left before she woke up in the mornings. He stayed busy at the CMO, wanting to give her space. A nanny helped some during the week, and

Rory got back into a routine of spending time at the library. Alandriel and Jimena were thankful Rory seemed to be thriving in her new situation.

Rory missed walking home with Quinn, but the two girls joined her now, and they would often stop to shop after work or eat at the International Café. Sometimes Jacoby showed up with members of the council for dinner meetings. He would always nod in her direction as the hostess escorted the group to one of the private rooms.

Jacoby had convinced the council to push his swearing-in ceremony and governor's ball out three more weeks. He needed time with Rory. He wanted her to be by his side. The council wasn't as hard to bend as he had anticipated. Colonel Lewis and Dr. Todd persuaded them further by suggesting the union would represent the coming together of all citizens in peace and respect.

Now Jacoby had to show Rory he was hers, if she would have him. It was time to seriously woo the woman he loved. The woman he had loved since the night they met. The woman who loved Jay as her own, who lay asleep three doors down the hall.

Thoughts of Rory kept him awake. Thoughts of the future. He heard little cries and jumped up to soothe his son. He flipped a lamp on and lifted Jay from his crib.

"Hello, baby. Wet, huh? Let's get you dry."

After changing him, he sat in the chair and rocked, but Jay still grunted.

"Hungry?"

Rory leaned on the door jamb. "Need a bottle?"

"I think so."

She looked beautiful padding across the carpet in her satin robe. She tucked her long waves behind her ears and smiled at him.

"Here." She handed him the bottle and bent down to kiss the tiny head. "There you go, my sweet."

Jay's bright green eyes watched her face.

"Rock a little more and he'll go right back to sleep."

The baby's eyes closed halfway as he took the last drops of milk.

"You're so good with him. You know exactly what to do, and he adores you. I'm so thankful you went to the brick yard that day," Jacoby whispered.

"Me too. Thank you for getting up with us tonight. It's nice."

"I want to do more for him ... and you." He gently laid Jay back down.

She looked bashful. "You know I don't mind."

He decided to take a chance, to be bold, and pulled her to the rocker and down onto his lap. It surprised her, but she didn't protest. She knew he had things on his mind. She played with his dark hair as he rocked them.

"What are you thinking about?" It was just like old times. Being near him was so easy and felt right again.

"We haven't had much time alone. I need you to know ... my feelings for you have never wavered, and I also know in my heart your time with Quinn was important. He needed you, and I wouldn't change anything that's happened. You've always been the stronger one between us. You make choices that are the best for you, and I admire that."

"Don't sell yourself short, Jake. You've made tough decisions, and you did it alone."

His eyes held hers, his face stone serious. "I don't want to anymore. Do it alone, I mean. I want you. I want you to be mine. I want us to be a real family. Just think about it."

She leaned her forehead against his and sighed, smiling. She touched her lips to his for a brief, sweet kiss and caressed his cheek, giving a bit of the energy he craved. Jacoby smiled back, knowing her heart.

❖❖❖❖❖❖❖

Over the next few days, the mansion buzzed with various council representatives touring the grounds and grand ballroom, making plans for the ball and dinner party. Sometimes Rory followed them around, listening and bouncing Jay on her hip.

Jacoby spent more time at home. They enjoyed dinners together and often took Jay to the study, where Rory read to him. It became Jacoby's favorite part of the night.

Dex and Alandriel joined them for dinner a couple of times a week.

"So, Rory and I want you two to sit at our table at the ball."

Alandriel lit up. "Oh wow! That's too nice of you! I still need to get a new dress."

Dex extended his hand to Jacoby. "We would be honored."

"I'll let the mercantile know you and Rory will be by tomorrow. Take Jimena too. Pick up new dresses, shoes, whatever else you women deem necessary. It's on me."

Rory covered his hand with hers. "Thank you, Jake."

"You'll be the prettiest girls there," he said with a wink.

❊❊❊❊❊❊

The trio met at the mansion to get ready together. Dex arrived well before the event was to begin to take pictures. Jacoby adored hearing the friends laughing on the staircase while he dressed in his tuxedo. Rory went to ask him if they could take some photos with Jay but stopped before entering his room. He stood in front of the long mirror adjusting his bow tie. Her body tingled. He looked so handsome. She remembered the day at the Crossroads, him looking like a prince after he'd had a shave. He still looked like a prince. It made her feel light inside, knowing he wanted to be her prince.

She noticed he caught sight of her in the reflection. Rory felt like a moon goddess in a long, midnight-blue gown that left her shoulders exposed. A feast for his eyes.

"Jake, you look wonderful."

He came to her, took her hands, and kissed her cheek. "No one will compare to you. I love hearing the sound of laughter in this big house."

"Come. We're being silly taking pictures. Can we get Jay in a few?"

"Yes, of course. I want one of the three of us."

They posed at the top of the stairs while the others watched Dex capture the moment. Orchestra music floated upward. Guests were beginning to mill around the ballroom.

"Gosh, you three look perfect," Jimena gushed.

Jacoby threw caution to the wind and bent down to steal a kiss. In response to Rory's questioning look, he whispered, "I don't care. They know I love you."

She looked at them.

Alandriel giggled. "We do."

Rory blushed and changed the subject. "I'll take Jay back to his room. We should get you to the ceremony."

Jacoby joined Colonel Lewis and Dr. Todd on the stage. The rest of the members filed in to sit in a row of wingback chairs. Rory and the others relaxed at the governor's table. The ambiance of the ballroom had a regal elegance, with round tables covered in bright white cloth and gardenia centerpieces. Half of the city was in attendance, and they slowly found their seats. Jacoby looked nervous.

The music faded, and Dr. Todd took the podium.

"Welcome to you, fine citizens of the Briar. This night has been a long time coming. Thank you all for your patience and support. The Briar has been through trying times. And we have been through triumphant times. We have experienced loss and tragedy but have been overall victorious and owe a great debt to Major General Jacoby Garrick. His reputation precedes him. His father was a highly honored military man.

The major general's bravery and good deeds remain unmatched. He is kind and accepting of his fellow officers, no matter their background or race. The council is confident, as I know the citizens are, of the decision to bestow upon Jacoby Garrick the title of governor."

Jacoby stood at attention facing the council members, who also stood.

"It is with great honor the council and I, as commissioner, present to you, citizens of the Briar, Governor Jacoby Garrick." Dr. Todd pinned a blue ribbon with a dangling brass medal to Jacoby's lapel. The new governor turned to the crowd, gave a humble bow, and winked at Rory.

Everyone stood, clapping, and the orchestra started back up with a jazzy number. Waiters and waitresses began serving the lavish dinner. Jacoby eventually made his way to join his friends after shaking several congratulatory gentlemen's hands at each table he passed.

He finally made it to his seat between Rory and Dex.

"That went perfectly. I'm so proud of you." Rory beamed.

"I wouldn't be here without you."

The group enjoyed the extravagant meal.

Colonel Lewis took the mic after most of the guests had finished dinner. "It is now time for the first dance, to be led by Governor Garrick, of course. Let's have a little fun, shall we?"

Jacoby scooted back from the table and held out his hand to Rory, who gladly took it. All eyes were on the pair, but no one seemed to care that she was a half. Their obvious connection couldn't be denied. The citizens had never seen the major general in such a joyous mood, and he looked at Rory with pure love. He held her with such care, and they passionately glided over the dance floor. Dex invited Alandriel to dance, starting to whirl her around to the beat of the music, followed by the other couples.

A slow, romantic tune floated through the air, and Jacoby slid his arm around Rory's waist, pulling her as close as possible. Her body reverberated against his. His lips brushed her earlobe, and he spoke lowly, "Rory none of this would matter if you weren't here with me."

She swooned and rested her cheek on his shoulder. When the music transitioned back to a jazzy mood, they went to the dessert table together and made light conversation with Dr. Todd, his wife—Mia—Dex, and Alandriel. Some of the gentlemen from the council approached and offered to take Jacoby to the court-yard for cigars and whiskey. Rory figured it was akin to an initiation of sorts. Jacoby kissed her cheek and went outside with them. Dex and Alandriel trotted back onto the dance floor, and Rory was left with Mia. She seemed nice, so Rory decided to get her opinion on something she had been worrying about.

"Mrs. Todd, can I ask you a question? Are there res-ervations in the council about Jacoby and me?"

She thought before speaking. "Can I tell you some-thing only Colonel Lewis, Theo, and I know because Jacoby shared it with us?"

"Please."

"At the attack ... on the Lark, Captain Barton made Jacoby promise him that he wouldn't leave you alone. That he would take care of you no matter what the council thought. But ... long before that, Jacoby had confided in my husband. The day he found out you married Quinn, he told Theo that he felt he had lost you. That you were his one true love, and he hoped the council would be okay with an unmarried governor because there would never be another love in his life like you."

Rory's eyes teared up, but she wiped them away before anyone could see. Mia touched her arm.

"So you see, Rory, the council believes you have brought light back into the governor's life. You have their full support if you choose to make anything official. Don't feel any pressure, though. You have to do what you've always done. Do what's best for you."

"Thank you, Mrs. Todd. You have eased my mind. I want what's best for the governor and the Briar."

The celebration went into the night, and Rory's feet started to hurt. The men and women of the council had migrated back to the governor's table and were talking city politics. Their glasses were empty, so Rory brought another round and served them.

There were all-around thanks, although she second-guessed her decision after seeing how intoxicated they were. Jacoby pulled her into his lap, surprising her. The group laughed. She kept her wits about her. Rory put her hands on his face and made him focus.

She spoke so only he could hear. "I'm tired. I'll check on Jay and then I'm going to bed. I suggest you wrap things up soon. I'll tell Vincent to make sure everyone gets home safe or spends the night in the guest wing."

He let go of her waist, and she got up. He grabbed her hand and kissed it. His eyes let her know that he had heard her loud and clear.

After speaking with Vincent and thanking the workers in the kitchen for making the night a success, she went to the nursery to let the nanny go home. It was after midnight, and Jay lay asleep, so she fell into the rocker and kicked off her heels.

Jacoby, meanwhile, headed to the kitchen, where Vincent handed him a glass of water and two pills to help stave off a hangover.

Rory thought about Jake. Her body ached to go find him, but she wanted him to be the hunter. Her lips longed to be kissed, and kissed thoroughly. The light from the hall went dark, and there stood his tall figure in the doorway. Her body tingled, and her heart raced. He glanced at the sleeping baby, then back to her. He indeed had found his prey. When he grinned, she stood but took her time getting to him.

"Where's your tie?"

"I have no idea."

He looked sleepy and sexy and wanting. His big hands gripped her small waist. She traced a finger over his lips and stood on tiptoe to taste his mouth. Her arms went around his neck, and his tongue worked magic. Her hands tugged at his hair, and his traveled down her to her bottom, where long fingers curled around to a very sensitive spot, eliciting a moan. He sucked on her neck, collarbone, then shoulder.

"Wait. We'll wake Jay."

He picked her up and carried her across the hall to his room. They looked at each other. After a moment, she turned around and pulled her hair over a shoulder to let him unzip her dress. He caressed her back and slowly pulled the tab down. She didn't move, standing bare before him.

Jacoby undressed with one hand while the other roamed her body. They had been close before but had never taken it this far. He had only dreamed of nights like this with her. He never thought it could become a reality, and now she was his.

Rory relished the attention he gave her. She turned around to look at the handsome man she had saved so long ago. Thoughts flew through her mind of his long legs hanging off the little bed in the cabin where she had thawed his body out. The memory of how their bodies vibrated together. It felt right now. They could enjoy each other. Be intimate with no holding back. No regrets. It was bittersweet, but fate had bestowed this gift on them. A future together.

She loved how he towered over her. He pulled her near, curled those big hands around her buttocks, and teased her again. He couldn't keep his mouth off her skin. Rory wanted more.

"Oh, Jake."

"My Rory. I love you."

"I love you."

He laid her down and unhurriedly pushed inside her. Her body quivered with intense vibrations, and he was so ready for her. He had always been ready for her. She saved his life every day she existed in his world. He took his time. Otherworldly sensations flowed through every pore, every cell. Melding into one took them to another level of arousal. Pleasure. Ecstasy. No one word could describe their mutual state of bliss. Their hips rocked together in a perfect rhythm, and when the climax came, a flood of satisfaction and contentment washed over them. Jacoby's tall body lay heavy on hers, but Rory delighted in the fact that she drove him wild, and she held on to him with her arms and legs. She didn't want him to ever leave her. He leaned up on one forearm to look at her face.

"Are we still on Earth? I swear we just went into another dimension."

She laughed a little. "Who cares where we are, my love."

He started to move, but she clamped on.

"No, don't. Stay. I like feeling you inside me. On top of me. All around me."

He kissed her neck and growled. "God, you are magic. I'd stay right here forever if we wouldn't eventually waste away into nothing. We could live off love for a while ..."

She laughed again. "Yes, for a while. I wonder what time it is. We've been up all night, I think."

"I bet the sun will be up soon. Why don't we get the nanny to come stay all day? I don't want to leave this room."

"Mmm. Yes. Sounds perfect."

Jacoby hopped up from the bed naked and spoke to Vincent through the communicator. Rory stretched and smiled, watching him. He returned to her snuggling under the covers.

"Remember Freywood castle? My feet were so cold. I still can't believe I have you here."

She shifted herself to lie across his chest, and he rubbed her back. "Jake, thank you for changing my life. I treasure every part of it."

"I told you I would always come back to you. I would never wish for you to go through such a loss. I want you to always know that, but I am thankful the universe kept you in my life, and I promise to always have you by my side from now on. The council knows how we feel about each other. They see that you make me a better man. A complete and utterly happy man."

Ripples of tranquility transferred from her hand to his as he laced their fingers together.

"And you have Jay. That appeases the council as well."

"We have Jay. He's just as much yours as he is mine."

A warm sensation overcame Rory as she thought about that precious little human. "I would give my life for him."

"I know you would, love."

"I think he feels my energy like you. I calm him so easily."

"The perfect mother." He laughed and kissed her hand.

"That sounds nice."

"Rory, if we didn't have Jay, you'd still be right here."

Like a lioness, she climbed on top to kiss his mouth and felt him wanting again.

"Yes. Now I belong to you."

"I don't own you."

Up to his ear she stalked, and purred, "I want you to." Her tongue licked his neck, teasing him.

Long fingers gripped her hips and sat her down in just the right place, filling her with his hard-on. "All right, love. Take all of me and give me your everything. Take me back to sweet euphoria."

He sat up and held her on his lap, and she rode him with zest. Long, wavy hair fell around her shoulders, and Rory displayed in full glory her eagerness to satisfy his every desire.

The two spent the day locked in Jacoby's room until sunset. Hunger finally persuaded the lovers to venture back to the present time. The clothing Rory needed still hung in her own closet, so she covered herself with the ball gown and ran across the hall to get dressed.

Adorable baby talk drifted down the hallway as Jacoby carried giggling Jay to Rory's room.

"Hello, baby. Hello, my love."

"We should move your things across the hall if you want."

"Mmm, yes. I would like that."

"Vincent said Jay has been up all day. I'm not tired. You've charged me up. We should go out to dinner, and there's a play tonight. I forgot it's Saturday."

"Oh, like a date?"

"Yes. I want to take you out."

Being with the governor had its perks. The driver let Jacoby and Rory out at a secret door at the rear of the International Café, and they were taken to a private room away from prying eyes. The head chef and owner brought out a bottle.

"This special sweet red is a gift for you, governor, and your beautiful companion. This table will always be reserved for you, sir."

He poured the wine, then retrieved dinner. The almost completely enclosed, circular booth allowed for such intimacy, and Jacoby's hands stayed distracted by Rory's knees and thighs as she fed him the most tender steak. Giddy and tipsy, Rory emptied the last drops of drink into her glass.

She bobbled a bit on the walk back to the car, and Jacoby helped her in. She climbed onto his lap and drunkenly kissed him during the ride to the theater. He enjoyed her pleasant blackberry wine taste and figured it might sober her up a little.

At the theater, citizens buzzed around the lobby like bees in a hive. Many eyes were on Jacoby and Rory as they slowly walked through the crowd of humans and halves, holding hands. He wished to show her off. Most greeted him with a nod or a "hello, governor."

The council members sat in the balcony at the top of a huge marble staircase. Theo and Mia were already seated, and Rory pulled on Jacoby's arm. "Jake, do I smell of wine?"

He laughed. "No. You smell like honeysuckle. My favorite."

Mia offered a warm smile, and they enjoyed the drama. Applause boomed as Evelyn and the rest of the cast took a bow at the end. Soon the throng meandered around, socializing. It seemed everyone wanted to greet and congratulate the new governor, and Rory proudly stood by his side. He introduced her to most, and she felt like a queen. Even the star of the show offered her respect.

"Evie." Jacoby kissed her cheek amicably.

"You look extremely delighted, Governor Garrick. I'm sincerely happy for you."

"I am on top of the world. Well done with the show, as always."

Evelyn turned to Rory. "Thank you for coming"—she leaned in close to Rory's ear—"and for loving Jake. He needs you. Also, I'm so sorry about Quinn. He is missed."

Rory hugged her. "Thank you, Evelyn."

All the conversing and smiling wore Rory out, and Jacoby pulled her into his lap again for the ride home.

"I'm sorry about all of that. I should have expected it my first night out as governor. Shouldn't be so bad next time."

"I don't really mind. Being with you is like being famous, isn't it? Are we expected to marry now?"

"No. I don't think so. Theo is the only member of the council who is married."

"I'll be honest. I'm afraid I may be cursed when it comes to marriage. I'm not sure I want to ever marry again."

"Well, I understand that. I'll never require anything of you, as long as you never leave me." His hold on her tightened. What little energy she had left to give exuded from her curled-up body.

"I couldn't. We are bound together. I am bound to you. I am bound to Jay, and I always will be."

EPILOGUE

How fast time flew by. Days turned into weeks. Weeks became months, and soon a year had passed. The Briar proved to be the most powerful colony in all the land. Humans from smaller cities migrated toward the outside edges of the Briar to sign treaties that provided security for them and expanded the borders of the colony. These land deals led to more crop and livestock growth, along with a boom in human pregnancies, which pleased the council.

The citizens held in highest regard their beloved governor and leader. More and more halves and humans had come together since Rory took her place at Jacoby's side. Dex and Alandriel married shortly after the ball and were expecting their first child in three months. His name would be Quinn if it was a boy and Lark if it was a girl.

No home had seen as much love as the governor's mansion. Jacoby held babbling Jay up straight and tall against the wall in his room as Rory marked where the top of his head touched. They laughed, and she wrote the year and his name so they could see how he would grow. The little one was into everything now, crawling about and pulling himself up on all of the furniture.

Jacoby let go, and Jay crawled into Rory's lap. Nap time had arrived. Jacoby smiled and touched the words she had written.

3001 – Jacoby Barton Garrick, Jr.

"He's going to be tall like his father." She kissed Jay's head and laid him in his bed. Jacoby took her hand and they went to the study. He chose a book from the shelf and sat on one end of the couch. Rory curled up next to him, and his long arm secured itself around her. She opened a notebook to the first clean page and began to write.

She poured herself out on the paper. Her pen spilled forth the words of her life. The story she would record was extraordinary. Future generations would know of Governor Jacoby Garrick's bravery and Captain Quinn Barton's sacrifice. Their acts of courage made the Briar a success, and she had a hand in that. She knew there would be so much more to tell. This was the new world.

PLAYLIST

Like I'm Gonna Lose You by Nicholas Yee

Sweet Jane by Cowboy Junkies

Come Away with Me by Norah Jones

Make You Feel My Love by Sleeping At Last

All I Want by Kodaline

Turning Page by Sleeping At Last

Here with Me by Susie Suh & Robot Koch

Lark by Parlor Hawk

Into Dust by Mazzy Star

Clair de Lune by Claude Debussy, Julian Lloyd Webber, Royal Philharmonic Orchestra, & Nicholas Cleobury

North by Sleeping At Last

The Night We Met by Lord Huron

Satellite Heart by Anya Marina

ACKNOWLEDGMENTS

First, I would like to thank my supportive and loving husband, Brian, and my mini-me, Alex Jane, for letting me sit and type for hours. They are my favorite humans on the planet.

Someone who I will never be able to thank enough is the experienced author and my friend, Thia Finn. She answers my many questions even late at night and on Sundays. Her advice will always be priceless to me. She encourages me with honesty and positivity. I am beyond grateful to have her on my side.

More thanks go out to my beta readers and feedback friends, Tonya Neely, Natalie Taylor Djerahian, and Alandriel Schnabel. I love them all and hope my stories continue to entertain them. Get ready. Another one is coming.

Another thank you goes out to my friends on social media. I adore them all for reading my random poetry and laughing at my weird attempts to be funny.

I have to shout the praises of my editor, Augustin Kendall. His hard work makes me look good, and my book is much better for it.

The glorious cover was made possible by Deranged Doctor Designs. Their team is simply amazing!

Finally, I give my love to the readers. You make the world a beautiful place with daydreaming and star wishing.

ABOUT THE AUTHOR

GINGER LEE, a lifelong Tennessee native, spent many years working as a surgical scrub technologist and surgical first assistant. She began writing at the age of thirty-six and spends her days raising her daughter, traveling with her husband, and attending concerts with friends.

To connect with Ginger Lee:

Amazon: https://www.amazon.com/
Ginger-Lee/e/B07PPVPKK6
Website: https://www.gleewrites.com
Email: gleewrites@gmail.com
Facebook: https://facebook.com/gingerweather
Instagram: https://www.instagram.com/gleewrites
Twitter: https://twitter.com/glee_writes

Made in the USA
Monee, IL
13 June 2020